# NURSERY RHYME THEME-A-SAURUS.

## The Great Big Book of Nursery Rhyme Teaching Themes

By **Jean Warren**

Illustrated by **Barb Tourtillotte**
Pattern Illustrations by **Judy Shimono**

**Totline® Publications**
A Division of Frank Schaffer Publications, Inc.
Torrance, California

Some of the activity ideas in this book were originally contributed by *Totline Newsletter* subscribers. We wish to acknowledge Marion Berry, Tacoma, WA; Valerie Bielsker, Lenexa, KS; Janice Bodenstedt, Jackson, MI; Paula Foreman, Lancaster, PA; Cathy B. Griffin, Plainsboro, NJ; Mildred Hoffman, Tacoma, WA; Colraine Pettipaw Hunley, Doylestown, PA; Joan Hunter, Elbridge, NY; Ellen Javernick, Loveland, CO; Wendy Kneeland, Incline Village, NV; Margery Kranyik, Hyde Park, MA; Linda Lehn, Pennsburg, PA; Joleen Meier, Marietta, GA; Rose Merenda, Warwick, RI; Kathy Monahan, Coon Rapids, MN; Ann M. O'Connell, Coaldale, PA; Sharon Olson, Minot, ND; Susan M. Paprocki, Northbrook, IL; Dawn Picolelli, Wilmington, DE; Lois E. Putnam, Pilot Mountain, NC; Polly Reedy, Elmhurst, IL; Betty Silkunas, Lansdale, PA; Diane Thom, Maple Valley, WA; Suzanne Thompson, Whittier, CA; and Bobbie Lee Wagman, Milton, WI.

*Editorial Manager:* Kathleen Cubley
*Editor:* Gayle Bittinger
*Copy Editor:* Brenda Mann Harrison
*Contributing Editors:* Elizabeth McKinnon, Linda Thomas
*Editorial Assistant:* Erica West
*Production Manager:* JoAnna Brock
*Art Director:* Jill Lustig
*Cover Design:* Eric Stovall
*Cover Illustration:* Carol DeBolt
*Book Design/Layout:* Sarah Ness

Theme-A-Saurus® is a registered trademark of Totline® Publications.

ISBN 0-911019-55-3

Library of Congress Catalog Card Number 92-60926
Printed in the United States of America
Published by: Totline® Publications

Business Office: 23740 Hawthorne Blvd.
Torrance, CA 90505

# Contents

# Introduction

Children love nursery rhymes. They are easy to remember because they tell stories and they rhyme. Sometimes as adults we forget that each new generation of children needs to be introduced to and immersed in these delightful rhymes.

Generally, we have included the original versions of the rhymes, but in a few cases, such as in "Peter, Peter Pumpkin Eater," we have deliberately changed the rhyme to reflect a more modern focus.

Nursery rhymes are a perfect medium from which to expand into mini-learning units. Interest is always high when reciting nursery rhymes, so capture this enthusiasm and extend it into expanded activities.

These rhymes can introduce art projects, give meaning to learning games, inspire movement activities or just provide lots of creativity and fun for both you and your children.

# The Gift of Rhyme

Share the wonder
Share the time,
Give your child
The gift of rhyme.

Give her words that hold a beat,
Fun to remember, fun to repeat.

Give her words that always flow,
Spoken fast or spoken slow.

Give her friends that entertain,
Give her words that never change.

Share the wonder
Share the time,
Give your child
The gift of rhyme.

*Jean Warren*

# Baa, Baa, Black Sheep

### Baa, Baa, Black Sheep

Baa, baa, black sheep,
Have you any wool?
Yes, sir, yes, sir,
Three bags full:
One for the master,
And one for the dame,
And one for the little boy
Who lives down the lane.

*Traditional*

### Black Sheep

Cut sheep shapes out of white construction paper, then cut black yarn into small pieces. Set out the sheep shapes, yarn pieces and glue. Let your children cover the sheep shapes with glued-on black yarn to make black sheep.

## Dyeing Yarn

Collect pieces of white yarn in various weights and textures from light, thin baby yarn to heavy, thick macrame cord. Heat water in an old saucepan and add one of the ingredients listed below, depending on the color desired. Bring the water to a boil. Then remove the pan from the heat and soak pieces of yarn in the water until the desired shade of color is reached. Squeeze the excess water out of the yarn and hang it to dry.

**yellow** — yellow or red onion skins
**green** — spinach
**purple** — blueberries
**red** — cranberries or beets
**blue** — red cabbage
**brown** — tea or walnut shells

## From Sheep to Clothes

Explain to the children how clothing is made. First the wool, or hair, of sheep is sheared off. The wool is combed to clean and prepare it for spinning. Then the wool is spun on a spinning wheel to make yarn. Next the yarn is put on a loom and woven to make cloth. Finally the cloth is cut and sewn to make clothes.

*Extension*: Draw a simple picture of each step on index cards. Mix up the cards and let your children take turns putting them in the right sequence. Encourage the children to describe each step to you.

## Flannelboard Fun

Photocopy the patterns on pages 10 and 11 and cut them out. If desired, cover them with clear self-stick paper. Attach felt strips to the backs of the patterns. As you recite the rhyme "Baa, Baa, Black Sheep," place the appropriate patterns on a flannelboard. Then let your children take turns putting the patterns on the flannelboard and reciting the rhyme.

## Counting Bags

Cut 10 bag shapes out of felt. Place some of the bags on a flannelboard. Have your children count the bags. Then take away a few of the bags and have the children tell you how many are left. Add some bags and have the children count them again. Repeat, taking away and adding bags as desired.

## Empty and Full

Give each of your children three empty lunch bags. Ask if the bags are empty or full. Give the children something to put in their bags (yarn, cotton balls, newspaper, etc.). When they each have "three bags full," say the rhyme "Baa, Baa, Black Sheep" together. Have them point to their bags, one at a time, as they recite the last four lines.

## Shearing Sheep

Have your children pair up. Ask one child in each pair to pretend to be the sheep and one child to pretend to be the shearer. Have the shearer shear the sheep. Then have all the children pretend to gather the wool and stuff it into bags. Collect the "bags of wool" from each pair of children and have them tell you how many full bags they have.

## First We Shear the Sheep
Sung to: "The Farmer in the Dell"

Oh, first we shear the sheep,
Oh, first we shear the sheep.
Heigh-ho, just watch us go,
Oh, first we shear the sheep.

Oh, next we comb the wool,
Oh, next we comb the wool.
Heigh-ho, just watch us go,
Oh, next we comb the wool.

Oh, then we spin the yarn,
Oh, then we spin the yarn.
Heigh-ho, just watch us go,
Oh, then we spin the yarn.

Oh, next we weave the cloth,
Oh, next we weave the cloth.
Heigh-ho, just watch us go,
Oh, next we weave the cloth.

From cloth we sew our clothes,
From cloth we sew our clothes.
Heigh-ho, just watch us go,
From cloth we sew our clothes.

*Jean Warren*

**10  Baa, Baa, Black Sheep**

**Baa, Baa, Black Sheep   11**

# Cobbler, Cobbler

### Cobbler, Cobbler

Cobbler, cobbler, mend my shoe,
Get it done by half past two;
Stitch it up and stitch it down,
Then I'll give you half a crown.

*Traditional*

### Lacing Shoes

Have a child place one of his or her shoes on a piece of posterboard. Trace around the shoe and cut out the shoe shape. Use a hole punch to punch holes around the edges of the shoe shape. Tie a long shoelace to one of the holes. Repeat for each child. Give the children their shoe shapes and let them use the laces to "stitch it up and stitch it down" to mend their shoes.

## Leather Art

Cut small purse and belt shapes out of leather scraps. Punch holes around the edges of the shapes. Thread plastic needles with yarn. Give a child a needle and one belt shape or two purse shapes. Show the child how to use the needle and thread to sew the purse shapes together or to make designs around the edges of the belt.

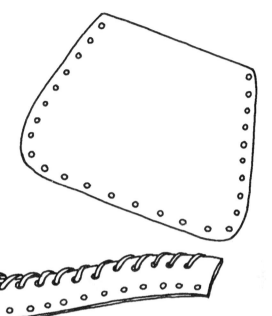

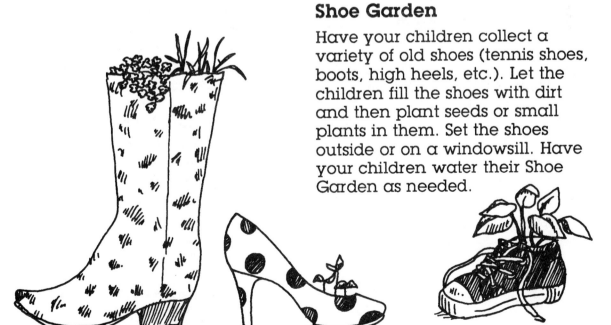

## Shoe Garden

Have your children collect a variety of old shoes (tennis shoes, boots, high heels, etc.). Let the children fill the shoes with dirt and then plant seeds or small plants in them. Set the shoes outside or on a windowsill. Have your children water their Shoe Garden as needed.

## Busy Little Cobbler

Use the shoe pattern on page 16 as a guide to cut a pair of shoes out of each of the following colors of felt: red, yellow, green, black and blue. As you read the poem below, place the appropriate colored shoes on a flannelboard.

Busy little cobbler,
With a cap upon your head,
Show me a pair of shoes
Colored red.

Busy little cobbler,
Such a happy fellow,
Show me a pair of shoes
Colored yellow

Busy little cobbler,
With shoes so clean,
Show me a pair of shoes
Colored green.

Busy little cobbler,
Hammering on a tack,
Show me a pair of shoes
Colored black.

Busy little cobbler,
Sewing up a shoe,
Show me a pair of shoes
Colored blue.

*Jean Warren*

## Flannelboard Fun

Photocopy the patterns on page 17 and cut them out. If desired, cover them with clear self-stick paper. Attach strips of felt to the backs of the patterns. Recite the "Cobbler, Cobbler" rhyme to your children and place the patterns on a flannelboard accordingly.

## Movement Fun

Read the "Cobbler, Cobbler" rhyme to your children. Then ask them to pretend to be cobblers. Tell them that you are bringing them shoes to fix, such as a heavy work boot, a pair of high heels, a sandal, a baby's shoe, etc. Have them show you how they would fix each one.

## Music Time

Sing the rhyme "Cobbler, Cobbler" to the tune of "The ABC Song." Or sing the song below and have your children pretend to make shoes.

Sung to: "The Muffin Man"

Do you know the busy cobbler,
The busy cobbler, the busy cobbler?
Do you know the busy cobbler
Who makes so many shoes?

He taps and taps all day long,
All day long, all day long.
He taps and taps all day long
And makes so many shoes.

*Jean Warren*

## Edible Crowns

In the rhyme "Cobbler, Cobbler," the cobbler was paid a half crown for the work. To make "crowns" you can eat, use the following recipe.

1 cup graham flour
1 cup whole-wheat flour
1/2 teaspoon *each* baking soda and salt
1/4 cup unsweetened apple-juice concentrate
1/4 cup vegetable oil
1 banana, sliced
1 teaspoon *each* vanilla and cinnamon

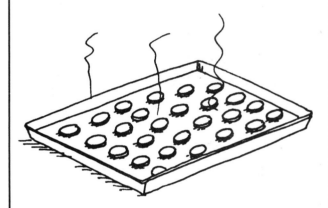

In a large bowl, stir together flours, baking soda and salt. Mix apple-juice concentrate, oil, banana, vanilla and cinnamon in a blender. Combine dry and liquid ingredients and mix thoroughly. Divide dough in half. Roll out each half on a floured surface until it is 1/8-inch thick. Use a small bottle lid, about 1 inch wide, to cut out circles. Bake on a cookie sheet at 350°F for 5 minutes.

**16    Cobbler, Cobbler**

# The Eensy, Weensy Spider

## The Eensy, Weensy Spider

The eensy, weensy spider
Went up the water spout,
Down came the rain
And washed the spider out.
Out came the sun
And dried up all the rain,
And the eensy, weensy spider
Went up the spout again.

*Traditional*

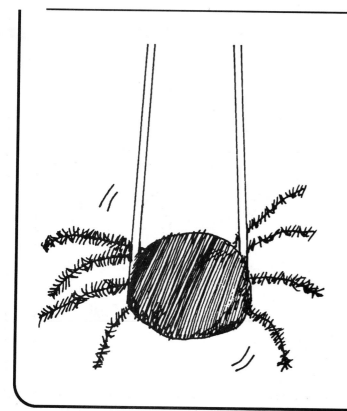

## Eensy, Weensy Spiders

Give each of your children a small piece of black playdough, eight short lengths of black pipe cleaners and a rubber band. Help each child form the playdough into a ball around one end of the rubber band. Then have the children poke the pieces of pipe cleaner into the playdough ball, four on each side, to make legs. Show the children how to make their spiders bounce up and down by holding onto the rubber bands.

## Spider Finger Puppets

Cut a 2-inch square out of black construction paper. Cut slits along the bottom half of the square. Wrap the square snugly around the tip of one of your children's fingers and tape it securely near the top. Fold the cut ends out to make spider legs. Make one for each child. Let the children use their spider puppets when they sing "The Eensy, Weensy Spider" or the song at right.

Sung to: "If You're Happy and You Know It"

There's a spider on my knee,
  on my knee.
There's a spider on my knee,
  on my knee.
There's a spider on my knee
And it sure is tickling me,
There's a spider on my knee,
  on my knee.

There's a spider on my nose,
  on my nose.
There's a spider on my nose,
  on my nose.
There's a spider on my nose,
It came up from my toes,
There's a spider on my nose,
  on my nose.

Let the children help you make up additional verses as desired.

*Adapted Traditional*

## Flannelboard Fun

Photocopy the patterns on pages 22 and 23 and cut them out. If desired, cover them with clear self-stick paper. Attach felt strips to the backs of the patterns. Read "The Eensy, Weensy Spider" rhyme to your children and place the patterns on a flannelboard accordingly.

## Counting Game

Draw a spider web on each of five paper plates. Number the webs from 1 to 5. Set out the webs and 15 plastic spiders. Let your children take turns placing the appropriate number of spiders on each web.

## One Little Spider

Take your children to a place where there are stairs or a safe ladder to climb. Have the children stand at the bottom of the stairs. Choose one child to start. Have that child pretend he or she is a spider that must climb the stairs. After the first child has climbed the stairs, have the child motion for another child to join him or her at the top. Continue until each child has climbed the stairs. If desired, recite the rhyme below as the children climb.

One little spider went out to play,
She climbed up a rain spout all the way.
She thought it was such a fabulous time,
She called for a friend to come and climb.

Another little spider went out to play,
He climbed up a rain spout all the way.
He thought it was such a fabulous time,
He called for another friend to come and climb.

*Jean Warren*

## Climb, Climb, Little Spider
Sung to: "Ten Little Indians"

Climb, climb, little spider,
Climb, climb, higher, higher.
Climb, climb, little spider,
Up the water spout.

Rain, rain falling down,
Rain, rain on the ground.
Rain, rain falling down,
Down the water spout.

Spider, spider falling down,
Spider, spider to the ground.
Spider, spider falling down,
Down the water spout.

Sun, sun shining bright,
Sun, sun bringing light.
Sun, sun shining bright,
On the water spout.

Climb, climb, little spider,
Climb, climb, higher, higher,
Climb, climb, little spider,
Up the water spout.

*Jean Warren*

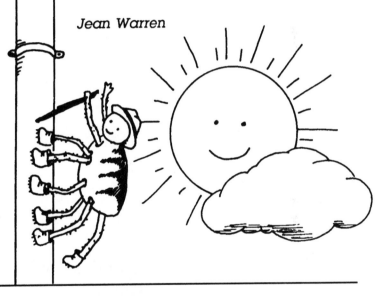

## Prune Spiders

Give each of your children a
large soft prune to use as a spider
body. Then let the children poke
pretzel sticks or crispy Chinese
noodles into the sides of their
prunes to make legs.

**22**   **The Eensy, Weensy Spider**

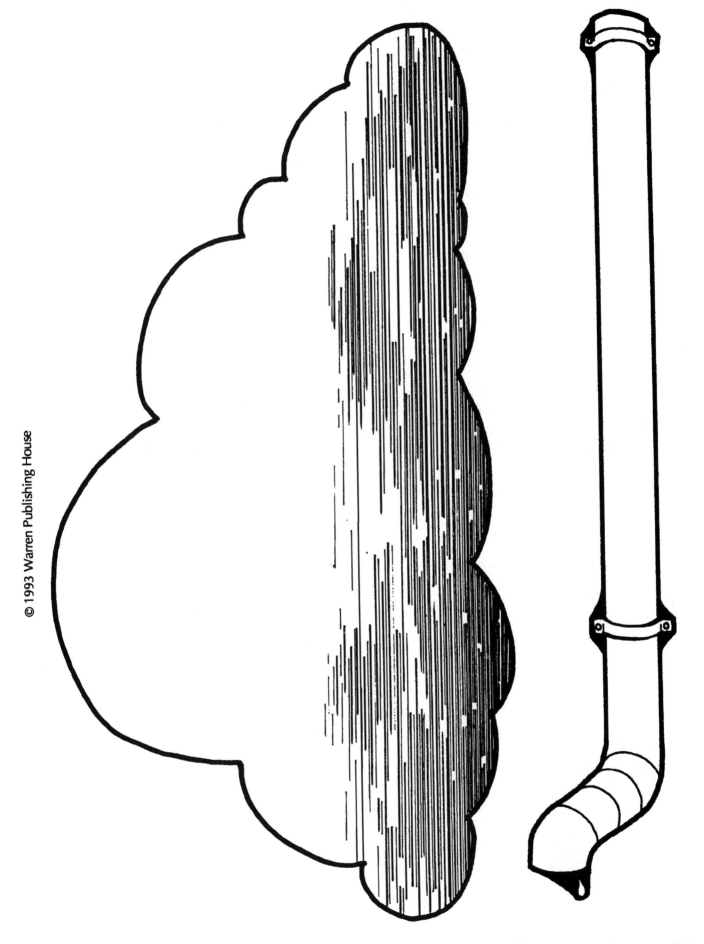

**The Eensy, Weensy Spider    23**

# Hickety, Pickety

## Hickety, Pickety

Hickety, pickety, my black hen,
She lays eggs for gentlemen;
Gentlemen come every day
To see what my black hen doth lay,
Sometimes nine and sometimes ten,
Hickety, pickety, my black hen.

*Traditional*

## Black Hens

For each child, cut a hen shape out of white construction paper, a nest shape out of brown construction paper, and 9 or 10 egg shapes out of white or tan construction paper (using the patterns on page 29 as guides). Let your children paint the hen shapes black. Allow the paint to dry. Have the children glue the hens on top of the nest shapes. Then have them glue the egg shapes on the nests. Let each child tell if his or her hen laid 9 or 10 eggs.

## Down at the Barnyard

Use the hen pattern on page 28 as a guide for cutting a hen shape out of each of the following colors of felt: black, red, yellow, brown and white. As you recite the poem below, put the appropriate colored hen on a flannelboard.

Down at the barnyard by the big corn sack,
Stood a little hen that was colored black.

Down at the barnyard by the kitten's bed,
Stood a little hen that was colored red.

Down at the barnyard by the iron bellow,
Stood a little hen that was colored yellow.

Down at the barnyard by the wagons for town,
Stood a little hen that was colored brown.

Down at the barnyard by the lantern bright,
Stood a little hen that was colored white.

*Jean Warren*

## Flannelboard Fun

Photocopy the patterns on page 29 and cut them out. If desired, cover them with clear self-stick paper. Attach felt strips to the backs of the patterns. Recite the rhyme "Hickety, Pickety" to your children and place the patterns on a flannel-board accordingly.

## Whose Nest?

Use the patterns on page 29 as guides for cutting five mother hen shapes out of black felt, five nest shapes out of brown felt and 15 egg shapes out of white felt. Cut numerals from 1 to 5 out of white felt and glue one on each hen shape. Glue a different number of eggs (from 1 to 5) in each nest shape. Place the nests and the mother hens on a flannelboard. Let your children help the mother hens find their nests by counting the eggs and matching each hen to the appropriate nest.

## Chicken, Chicken

Have the children sit in a semi-circle. Place a chair in front of the semicircle, facing away from the children. Choose one child to be the Chicken and have him or her sit in the chair. Place a plastic egg under the chair. Quietly choose one child to "steal" the egg from the Chicken and sit back down in the semicircle, holding the egg behind his or her back. Then have all the children put their hands behind their backs and pretend to have the egg. When the children chant "Chicken, Chicken, who has your egg?" have the Chicken turn around and begin guessing who might have it. When the Chicken guesses correctly, let the child with the egg be the new Chicken.

## How Many Eggs?

Make a nest out of a plastic basket, cardboard box or pillow. Put from none to 10 plastic eggs on the nest. Ask a child to pretend to be a hen and sit on the nest without looking at the eggs. Have the hen guess how many eggs are in the nest. Then help the hen count the eggs. Repeat for each child.

## See the Little Black Hens
Sung to: "Down by the Station"

Down at the barnyard
Early in the morning,
See the little black hens
Standing in a row,
Counting all their eggs,
Clucking as they go.
Cluck-cluck, cluck-cluck,
Off they go.

*Jean Warren*

## Cooking Eggs-Periments

Show a carton of eggs to your children. Ask them to think of different ways to cook the eggs. Then let your children help you prepare the eggs in three or four ways, such as hard-boiled, scrambled, in an omelette and fried. Give each child a small amount of each type of cooked egg on a plate. As the children eat their eggs, ask questions such as these: "Which egg do you like the best? The least? How was your favorite egg cooked? Which one is the hardest? What is an egg like before it's cooked? After it's cooked?"

**28**  **Hickety, Pickety**

# Hickory, Dickory, Dock

## Hickory, Dickory, Dock

Hickory, dickory, dock,
The mouse ran up the clock.
The clock struck one,
The mouse ran down,
Hickory, dickory, dock.

*Traditional*

## Paper Plate Clocks

Give each of your children a paper plate and a long and a short strip of black construction paper. Let the children examine the hands of a real clock. Then have them glue their paper strips to their paper plates to make clock hands. Help your children use felt-tip markers to write numerals on their clocks.

Then cut simple mouse shapes out of gray construction paper. Give each child one of the mice and a piece of gray yarn for a tail. Have each child glue the tail to his or her mouse shape. Then let the children glue their mouse shapes anywhere on their clocks.

## A Little Mouse

Read the following poem to your children. Encourage them to say the rhyming words as you go along.

A little mouse ran up the clock
He thought that it was fun,
But when he reached the very top
The clock struck one.

Another mouse ran up the clock
In tiny shoes of blue,
And when she reached the very top
The clock struck two.

Another mouse ran up the clock
To see what he could see,
And when he reached the very top
The clock struck three.

Another mouse ran up the clock
And found a little door,
And when she reached the very top
The clock struck four.

*Jean Warren*

## Flannelboard Fun

Photocopy the patterns on page 34 and cut them out. If desired, cover them with clear self-stick paper. Attach felt strips to the backs of the patterns. Place the patterns on a flannelboard. As you recite the "Hickory, Dickory, Dock" rhyme, let your children take turns moving the mouse up and down the clock.

## Clock Corner

Set out several different types of clocks (digital, alarm, wind-up, etc.). If you have a sundial, put it outside for your children to see on a sunny day. Let the children play with the clocks. Show the children how to set the clocks to one o'clock. If desired, set the alarms on the clocks to go off at one o'clock.

## Clock Lotto Game

Make two photocopies of the Clock Lotto Game board on page 35. Glue each photocopy to a piece of posterboard. Cut one game board into cards. Cover the cards and the remaining game board with clear self-stick paper for durability, if desired. Let your children take turns placing the game cards on top of the matching pictures on the game board.

## Nine Little Mice

Sung to: "Ten Little Indians"

*Sing slowly:*

One little, two little, three little mice,
Four little, five little, six little mice,
Seven little, eight little, nine little mice,
All crept up the clock.
BONG!

*Sing quickly:*

One little, two little, three little mice,
Four little, five little, six little mice,
Seven little, eight little, nine little mice,
All ran home to bed!
Shhh.

*Jean Warren*

## Music Time

Sing "Hickory, Dickory, Dock" with the children. Give rhythm sticks and wood blocks to some of the children to tap out the clock rhythm. Give triangles to others to strike the hour chime.

## Clock Snacks

Use rice cakes or bread cut into circles for clock faces. Spread with peanut butter. Place raisins or small pieces of fruit around the edges of the crackers to represent numerals. Use carrot or celery sticks to represent hands of a clock at the one o'clock position.

**34** Hickory, Dickory, Dock

# Humpty Dumpty

## Humpty Dumpty

Humpty Dumpty sat on a wall,
Humpty Dumpty had a great fall.
All the king's horses and all the king's men,
Couldn't put Humpty together again.

*Traditional*

## Humpty Dumpty Art

Cut plastic foam eggs in half lengthwise. Cut rectangles out of construction paper. Set out the egg halves, the rectangles, large pieces of construction paper, and various materials for decorating the plastic foam eggs, such as wallpaper scraps, yarn, beads, felt-tip markers, etc. Have each of your children glue a rectangle to a piece of construction paper for a wall and an egg half on top of the wall. Then let them use the decorating materials to make faces on their eggs. To finish, give each child two 1- by 8-inch strips of construction paper to accordion-fold and glue on as legs. Display the artwork on a wall or a bulletin board. If desired, write the poem on a separate piece of paper to display with the art.

## Rhymes

Ask your children to think of other things that Humpty Dumpty might have sat on. Then recite the first line of the poem, pausing when you get to the end of the line. Have one of your children name something that Humpty might have sat on. Then change the next line to rhyme with the word the child said. End the rhyme as usual. An example follows.

Humpty Dumpty sat on a horse,
Humpty Dumpty fell off, of course.
All the king's horses and all the king's men,
Couldn't put Humpty together again.

*Extension*: Have each child draw a picture of what he or she thinks Humpty Dumpty sat on. Then write the new version of the rhyme on the child's paper.

## Egg Fall

Have your children work together to build a wall of blocks. Place a container at the bottom of the wall. Put a raw egg on the top of the wall. Ask the children to guess what will happen when the egg falls off the wall and into the container. Then push the egg off the wall. Can the children tell you why all the king's men couldn't put Humpty together again?

## Flannelboard Fun

Photocopy the patterns on pages 40 and 41 and cut them out. Cut the Humpty Dumpty pattern in half as indicated by the dotted line. If desired, cover the patterns with clear self-stick paper. Attach felt strips to the backs of the patterns. Cut a rectangular wall shape out of felt. Place the wall on a flannelboard. Put Humpty Dumpty together and arrange him on top of the wall. Recite the rhyme, having Humpty Dumpty fall off the wall and "break" into two pieces. Then place the king's horses and king's men on the flannelboard as they are mentioned.

## Counting Rhyme

Make five photocopies of the Humpty Dumpty pattern on page 41 and cut them out. If desired, cover them with clear self-stick paper. Attach strips of felt to the backs. Cut a long wall shape out of felt. Place the wall shape and the five Humpty Dumpty patterns on a flannelboard. As you recite the poem below, remove the Humpty Dumpty patterns one at a time.

Five Humpty Dumpties,
And not one more,
One dropped to the ground
And then there were four.

Four Humpty Dumpties,
Cute as they could be,
One did a flip-flop
And then there were three.

Three Humpty Dumpties,
Just a lonely few,
Down went another one
And then there were two.

Two Humpty Dumpties,
Basked in the sun,
One got baked
And then there was one.

One Humpty Dumpty,
A real egg-head hero,
He took a mighty fall
And then there were zero.

*Susan M. Paprocki*

## Poor Humpty Dumpty
Sung to: "Three Blind Mice"

Poor Humpty Dumpty,
Poor Humpty Dumpty.
It's sad to tell
That he broke his shell.
He hurried and scurried to the top of the wall,
He sat on the edge and had a great fall,
But he couldn't bounce like a rubber ball,
Poor Humpty Dumpty.

*Ann M. O'Connell*

## Humpty Dumpty Shapes

Cut the following shapes out of felt: one large oval (Humpty Dumpty), one large rectangle (wall), two small circles (eyes), one small triangle (nose), one medium triangle (hat), one small oval (mouth). Set out the shapes and let your children take turns arranging them on a flannelboard to "put Humpty Dumpty together again." Encourage the children to name the shapes as they use them.

## Humpty Dumpty Eggs

Give your children large baby food jars. Help each child crack an egg into his or her jar, then add 1 teaspoon milk and 1 teaspoon cottage cheese. Have the children shake their jars. Lightly grease muffin tins and pour each child's mixture into a muffin tin cup. Bake at 350°F until the eggs start to cook. Take out the muffin tins, stir each egg once and return the tins to the oven until the eggs are set. Serve on toast.

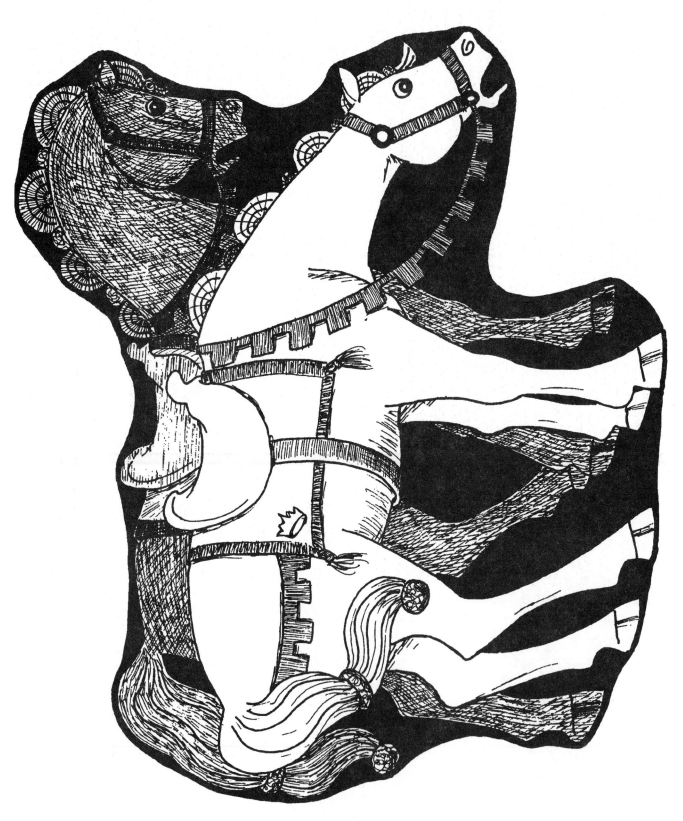

**40** Humpty Dumpty

# Jack and Jill

## Jack and Jill

Jack and Jill
Went up the hill,
To fetch a pail of water.
Jack fell down
And broke his crown,
And Jill came tumbling after.

*Traditional*

## Water Colors

Make water-color paint for your children by pouring various colors of leftover tempera paint into the egg cups of plastic foam egg cartons. Allow the paint to dry. Cut each egg carton into thirds. Give each of your children one of the sections, a brush, a cup of water and a piece of paper. Then let them make water-color pictures.

## Experimenting With a Pulley

Hang a pulley from the ceiling. Put a rope through the pulley and tie a plastic bucket to one end of the rope. Tell your children about the pulley and how Jack and Jill might have used a pulley to help them get water from the well. Then let your children take turns lowering the bucket to the floor, having it filled with "water" and raising the bucket.

## Flannelboard Fun

Photocopy the patterns on pages 46 and 47 and cut them out. If desired, cover the patterns with clear self-stick paper. Attach strips of felt to the backs of the patterns. Cut a hill shape out of felt. Arrange the patterns on a flannelboard. As you recite the "Jack and Jill" rhyme, move the patterns accordingly.

## Opposites Matching Game

Cut out magazine pictures of things that are opposites, such as a full glass and an empty glass, a boy and a girl, a flat road and a curved hill. Glue each picture to an index card. If desired, cover the cards with clear self-stick paper for durability. Mix up the cards and let your children take turns matching the opposites.

## Water Relay

Divide your children into two teams. Place two buckets of water on one side of the room and two identical empty jars on the other side. Have each team stand by one of the water buckets. Give the first child in each team a paper cup. When you say "Go," have the children with the cups fill them with water, carefully walk to the empty jars, pour their water into the jars, then hurry back and give their cups to the next children in line. Continue until each child has had a turn or until a designated time is up. When the relay is finished, see how much water is in each jar.

## When I Got Water Today
Sung to: "The Paw-Paw Patch"

Scooped up water, then put it in my bucket,
Scooped up water, then put it in my bucket,
Scooped up water, then put it in my bucket,
When I got water from the well today.

Dropped my bucket, then rolled down the hill,
Dropped my bucket, then rolled down the hill,
Dropped my bucket, then rolled down the hill,
When I got water from the well today.

Have your children act out the movements
described in the song.

*Jean Warren*

## Jack and Jill Log Rolls

Take your children to a grassy
slope or hill. Recite or sing the
rhyme "Jack and Jill." Have the
children do log rolls down the hill
when you get to the line "Jack
fell down."

## Ladling Water

Set out a clean bucket filled with
water, a ladle and some cups. At
snacktime, have each of your
children use the ladle to fill a cup
with water from the bucket.

**46   Jack and Jill**

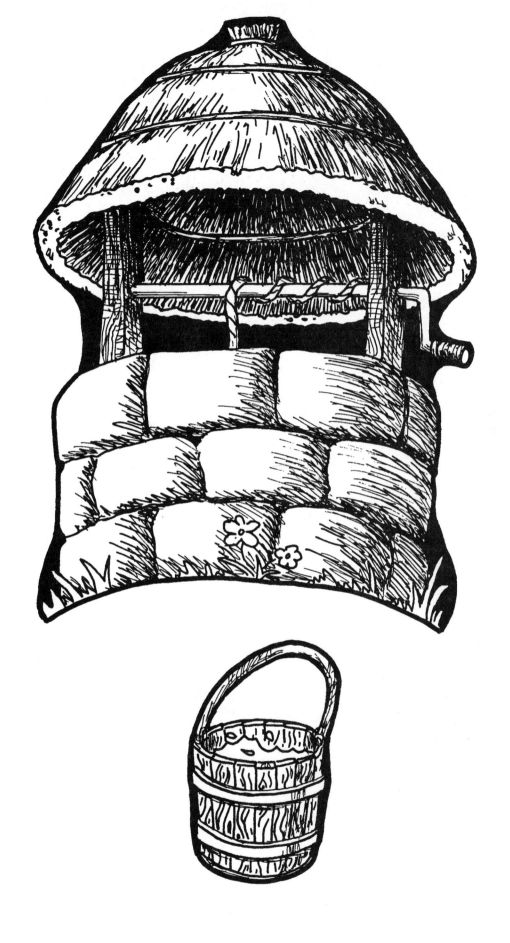

# Jack Be Nimble

### Jack Be Nimble

Jack be nimble,
Jack be quick;
Jack jump over
The candlestick.

*Traditional*

## Candle Printing

Give your children various shapes and kinds of candles. Let them dip the candles into paint and use them to make prints on pieces of construction paper. Encourage the children to print with the bottoms and the sides of their candles.

## Candle in a Jar

Set out a votive candle (or other small candle) and a jar that is just large enough to fit over it. Light the candle. Ask your children to guess what will happen when you put the jar over the top of the candle. Put the jar over the candle. In a short time the flame will go out. Let your children guess why the flame went out. (The flame needs oxygen to burn and when the jar is put over it, no more oxygen can get to it.)

## Candle Puppets

Give each child a toilet tissue tube. Set out brushes and several different colors of tempera paint. Let the children paint their toilet tissue tubes any color they wish. When the paint has dried, give each child a tongue depressor and a yellow construction-paper flame shape. Have the children glue their flame shapes to the tops of their tongue depressors. Then show the children how to "light" their candle puppets by pushing their tongue depressor flames up through their painted cardboard tubes.

## Flannelboard Fun

Photocopy the patterns on page 52 and cut them out. If desired, cover them with clear self-stick paper. Attach strips of felt to the backs of the patterns. Place the patterns on a flannelboard. Recite the rhyme "Jack Be Nimble" with your children and move the patterns accordingly.

## Matching Game

Make two photocopies of the game cards on page 53. Cut out the cards and, if desired, cover them with clear self-stick paper for durability. Mix up the cards and let your children take turns finding the matching pairs.

## Candle Games

**Color Game** — Let your children sort a variety of large birthday candles by color. Then have them count how many candles of each color there are.

**Number Game** — Label five boxes or other containers from 1 to 5. Set out 15 candles. Let your children take turns placing the appropriate number of candles in each box.

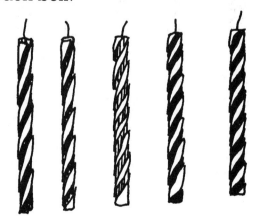

## Jumping Games

Have your children recite the rhyme "Jack Be Nimble" as they do a variety of jumping activities. A rope or a strip of tape on the floor is easy to jump over. Practice big and little jumps, tall and short jumps, quiet and loud jumps. Jumping off something is lots of fun and safe if there are soft pillows to land on and an adult to supervise one-at-a-time jumping. As each child jumps, say the rhyme with his or her name in place of *Jack*.

## Candle Salads

To make each salad, place a pineapple ring on top of a lettuce leaf. Stand half of a peeled banana upright in the center of the pineapple ring. Cut off the pointed end of the banana. Use a vegetable peeler to peel off a strip of carrot. Roll the carrot strip into a ring, overlapping the ends. Stick one end of a toothpick through the ends of the carrot strip and one end down into the banana. Pinch the carrot ring to make it look like a pointed candle flame.

## Once There Was a Boy Named Jack
Sung to: "Twinkle, Twinkle, Little Star"

Once there was a boy named Jack,
He loved to jump over and back.
He jumped over candles,
He jumped over sticks,
He loved to do his jumping tricks.
Once there was a boy named Jack,
He loved to jump over and back.

*Jean Warren*

**52** **Jack Be Nimble**

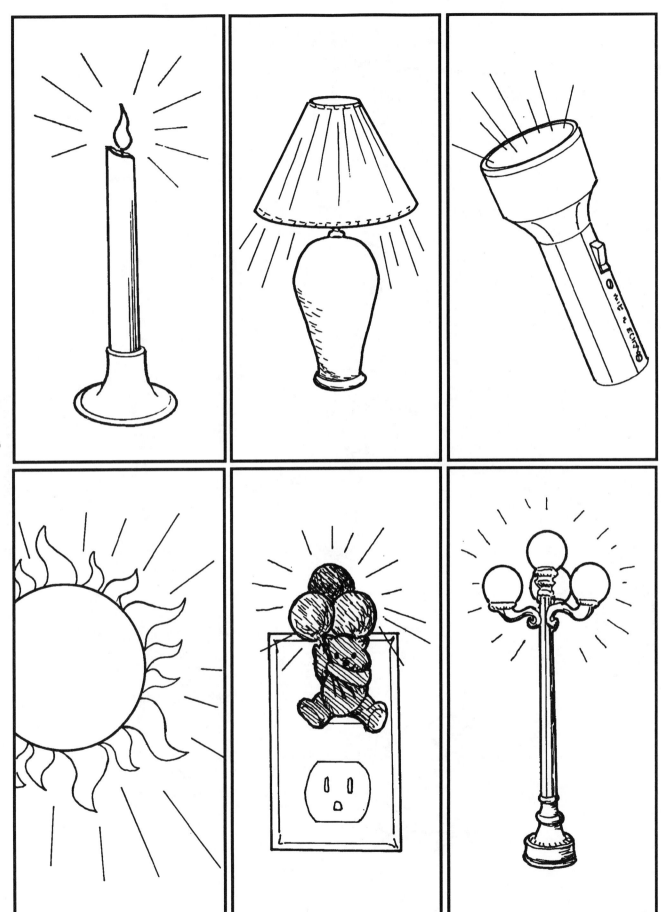

**Jack Be Nimble** 53

# Little Boy Blue

## Little Boy Blue

Little Boy Blue,
Come blow your horn,
The sheep's in the meadow,
The cow's in the corn;
But where is the boy,
Who looks after the sheep?
He's under a haystack
Fast asleep.

*Traditional*

## Under the Haystack Art

Give each of your children a piece of construction paper with a photocopy of the Little Boy Blue pattern from page 58 glued on it. Have the children glue short pieces of straw or any kind of dried grass over Little Boy Blue so that he will be "under the haystack."

*Variation:* Instead of straw, use pieces of yellow or tan yarn.

## Blue Day

Have a Blue Day with your children. Ask them to wear blue and bring blue things to share. Let them paint pictures of the blue sky. Count how many of them have blue eyes. Use blue aquarium gravel for sandbox play. Cut and fold blue paper. Take a walk to mail letters in a blue mailbox.

## Flannelboard Fun

Photocopy the Little Boy Blue, cow and sheep patterns on pages 58 and 59 and cut them out. Cover them with clear self-stick paper, if desired. Attach felt strips to the backs of the patterns. Use the haystack pattern on page 58 as a guide for cutting a haystack shape out of yellow felt. Place the sheep and the cow on one side of a flannelboard. Place Little Boy Blue on the other side with the haystack on top of him. Read the rhyme "Little Boy Blue" to your children and let them discover Little Boy Blue fast asleep under the haystack.

## Counting Song

Make nine photocopies of the sheep and cow patterns on page 59 and cut them out. If desired, cover them with clear self-stick paper. Attach felt strips to the backs of the patterns. As you sing the first two verses of the following song, place the sheep and cows on the flannelboard one at a time. Then sing the third verse. Finally remove the sheep and cows, one at a time, as you sing verses four and five. Sing the song again and let your children help you put on and take off the sheep and cows.

Sung to: "Ten Little Indians"

One little, two little,
Three little sheep,
Four little, five little,
Six little sheep,
Seven little, eight little,
Nine little sheep,
Playing in the meadow.

One little, two little,
Three little cows,
Four little, five little,
Six little cows,
Seven little, eight little,
Nine little cows,
Playing in the corn.

Little Boy Blue
Come blow your horn,
Little Boy Blue
Come blow your horn,
Little Boy Blue
Come blow your horn,
Call them all back home.

One little, two little,
Three little sheep,
Four little, five little,
Six little sheep,
Seven little, eight little,
Nine little sheep,
Heading now for home.

One little, two little,
Three little cows,
Four little, five little,
Six little cows,
Seven little, eight little,
Nine little cows,
Heading now for home.

*Jean Warren*

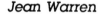

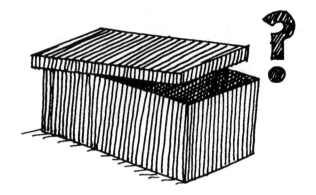

## Little Boy Blue's Box

Cover a box with blue construction paper. Hide a blue object, such as a blue hat, a blue button or a blue crayon, inside the box. Show your children the box. Tell them that Little Boy Blue has put something blue in the box. Then give them clues about the object until they guess what it is.

## Music and Drama

Have your children act out the motions described as you sing the following song about Little Boy Blue.

Sung to: "Twinkle, Twinkle, Little Star"

Little Boy Blue, come blow your horn,
    (Pretend to blow horn.)
The sheep's in the meadow, the cow's in the corn.
    (Point to the right, then to the left.)
Where's the boy who looks after the sheep?
    (Cup hand over eye and look around.)
He's under the haystack, fast asleep.
    (Pretend to sleep.)
Little Boy Blue, come blow your horn,
    (Pretend to blow horn.)
The sheep's in the meadow, the cow's in the corn.
    (Point to the right, then to the left.)

*Adapted Traditional*

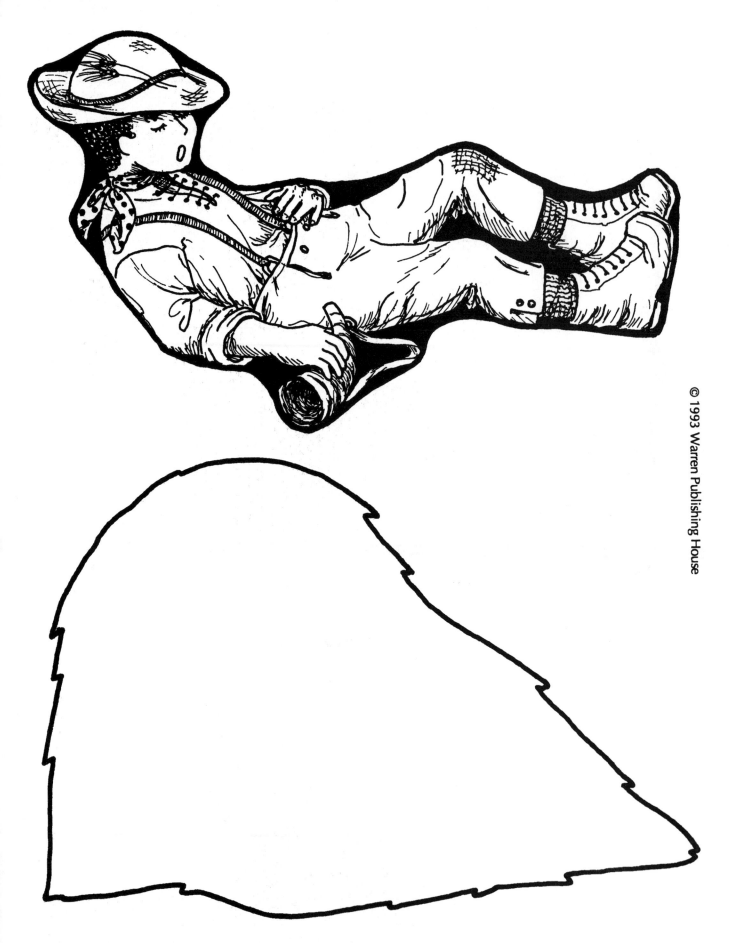

**58** **Little Boy Blue**

# Little Miss Muffet

## Little Miss Muffet

Little Miss Muffet
Sat on a tuffet,
Eating her curds and whey;
There came a big spider,
Who sat down beside her
And frightened Miss Muffet away.

*Traditional*

## Thumbprint Spiders

Fold paper towels in half, place them in shallow containers and pour on small amounts of black tempera paint to make paint pads. Give each child a piece of white construction paper. Have the children press their thumbs onto the paint pads and then onto their papers to make prints. Let them make as many prints as they like. When the paint is dry, have the children add eight legs to each of their thumbprints with black felt-tip markers to make spiders.

## Making a Spider Web

Show the children a real spider web or a picture of one. Talk about the shape of the web. Tell the children that spiders make webs to catch the insects that they eat. Then let the children make their own giant web out of yarn. Have the children sit in a circle. Give a large ball of yarn to one child. Have that child hold the end of the yarn and gently toss the ball of yarn to another child. Have that child hold the yarn and toss the ball to another child. Repeat until each child is holding a section of the yarn and the web is complete. Then ask the children what they would like to catch in their web.

## Flannelboard Fun

Photocopy the patterns on page 65 and cut them out. If desired, cover the patterns with clear self-stick paper. Attach strips of felt to the backs of the patterns. Place Miss Muffet on a flannelboard. Point out the tuffet and the bowl of curds and whey to your children. Then recite the "Little Miss Muffet" rhyme, moving the patterns accordingly.

## Body Parts Rhyme

Give each child a plastic spider ring (available in bulk at variety stores). Recite the following rhyme and have the children move their spiders as directed.

The teeny tiny spider
Began to crawl on me,
I found him on my leg,
To be exact, my knee.

The teeny tiny spider
Crawled up onto my chest,
This was such a long trip,
He took a little rest.

The teeny tiny spider
Headed for my arm,
It tickled quite a bit,
But I knew he meant no harm.

The teeny tiny spider
Crawled up on my finger,
He landed on my thumb,
But he didn't want to linger.

I helped him to my face
And placed him on my nose,
Then he lost his balance,
And fell down to my toes.

The teeny tiny spider
Went upon his way,
He clearly had enough,
Of his crawling for today.

*Susan M. Paprocki*

## Talking About Fears

Talk about how Little Miss Muffet was frightened by the spider. Then encourage the children to discuss the things that frighten them. Be careful not to belittle them for having fears. Let them know that we are all afraid of something. Ask the children if they can think of ways to handle their fears.

## Which Spider?

Fill eight small paper bags with newspaper and tie the tops closed with string or yarn. Turn the bags upside down and draw a simple spider face on each one. Tape a different number of crepe paper spider legs (from 1 to 8) to each bag. Make a yarn "hanger" for the top of each bag. Place a "tuffet" or stool in the middle of the room and ask your children to sit around it. Have one child sit on the stool and pretend to be Little Miss Muffet. As you recite the rhyme, lower one of the bag spiders down beside the child. Ask the other children to tell you which spider "sat down beside her" by counting the number of legs on the spider. Then let Little Miss Muffet select another child for the next turn.

## Counting Eight

Show your children a real spider or a picture of one. Have them count the number of legs on the spider. Then set out a variety of small objects such as marbles, cotton balls or crayons. Let your children use the objects to make sets of eight.

## Miss Muffet Game

Divide the children into two groups. Have one group pretend to be Miss Muffets and sit on chairs. Have the other group pretend to be Spiders. As you sing the first verse of the following song, have the Miss Muffets pretend to eat their curds and whey. As you sing the first three lines of the second verse, have each Spider stand by a Miss Muffet. On the last line, have the Spiders scare the Miss Muffets and make them run away. Then have the Spiders and the Miss Muffets switch roles.

Sung to: "Oh, My Darling Clementine"

I'm Miss Muffet, I'm Miss Muffet,
I'm Miss Muffet now today.
I'm Miss Muffet on my tuffet,
Eating all my curds and whey.

I'm the Spider, I'm the Spider,
I'm the Spider now today.
I'm the Spider just beside her,
I will make her run away.

*Lois E. Putnam*

## Curds and Whey

Warm 2 cups whole milk and add 1 teaspoon vinegar. Stir as the curds separate from the whey. (Curds are milk solids and whey is the liquid. You can let the children taste the whey, but they probably won't care for it.) Strain the curds, place them between paper towels and press out the excess liquid. Serve the curds chilled as cottage cheese. Or whip the curds until smooth, stir in cinnamon, vanilla or peanut butter and use the mixture as a spread for crackers.

**Little Miss Muffet   65**

# Mary Had a Little Lamb

### Mary Had a Little Lamb

Mary had a little lamb,
Its fleece was white as snow;
And everywhere that Mary went,
The lamb was sure to go.

It followed her to school one day,
Which was against the rule;
It made the children laugh and play,
To see a lamb at school.

*Traditional*

### Cotton Ball Lambs

For each child, cut a lamb body shape out of white posterboard or lightweight cardboard, using the pattern on page 71 as a guide. Have your children use black felt-tip markers to draw facial features on their lamb shapes. Then let them glue cotton balls all over the bodies of the lambs to make "fleece as white as snow." When the glue has dried, clip two spring-type clothespins on the bottom of each shape to make legs for the fluffy lambs to stand on.

## Mary and Her Lambs

Cut several tongue depressors in half. Glue each half onto the middle of a paper plate. With a permanent felt-tip marker, draw Mary's face near the top of each tongue depressor. Let your children glue scraps of yarn or curly ribbon for hair and scraps of fabric, construction paper or tissue paper for clothing onto their tongue depressors. Let them add curved pipe-cleaner "staffs" and cotton-ball "sheep" to their Mary and Her Lambs scenes.

*Variation*: For a simpler project, just have your children glue cotton-ball "sheep" to pieces of construction paper.

## Pet Surveys

Make a form for your children to use when conducting this Pet Survey. Print the question "What kinds of pets do you have?" at the top of a piece of paper. Down the left-hand side of the paper, draw and label pictures that show the most likely responses to the question such as a cat, dog, fish, bird and hamster. Make a copy for each child. Then attach the surveys to clipboards and hand them out to the children. Let the children interview one another and record answers to the survey question by making check marks next to the appropriate pictures on their survey forms. Later, arrange a time for the children to share the results of their pet surveys.

## Pet Questions

Discuss with your children what they would do if their pets followed them to school. Ask them questions such as these: "Where would your pets wait for you? What would you do if your pets wanted to play? When would your pets eat?"

## Flannelboard Fun

Photocopy the patterns on page 70 and cut them out. If desired, cover the patterns with clear self-stick paper. Attach felt strips to the backs of the patterns. Place the patterns on a flannelboard. Recite the rhyme "Mary Had a Little Lamb" with your children, moving the patterns accordingly.

## Follow the Leader

Use the rhyme "Mary Had a Little Lamb" as a transitional song. Let your children take turns being Mary and have the rest of the children follow him or her out to play, to snack or to circle time, wagging their "tails" behind them.

## A Lamb at School
Sung to: "Little White Duck"

There's a little white lamb,
Who goes to school each day.
A little white lamb
Who likes to work and play.
Watch him nibble all the books,
And in each lunch he will surely look.
There's a little white lamb,
Who goes to school each day
Baa, baa, baa.

*Jean Warren*

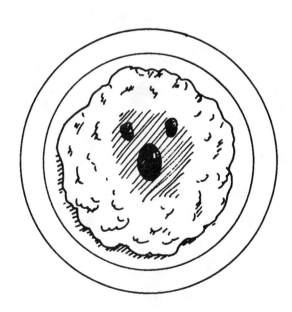

## Salad Lambs

To make each salad lamb, place a mound of cottage cheese in the middle of a small plate. Flatten it with the back of a spoon and make a hollow in the center for the lamb's face. Let the children add raisins for eyes and halves of red grapes or cherry tomatos for noses.

**70** Mary Had a Little Lamb

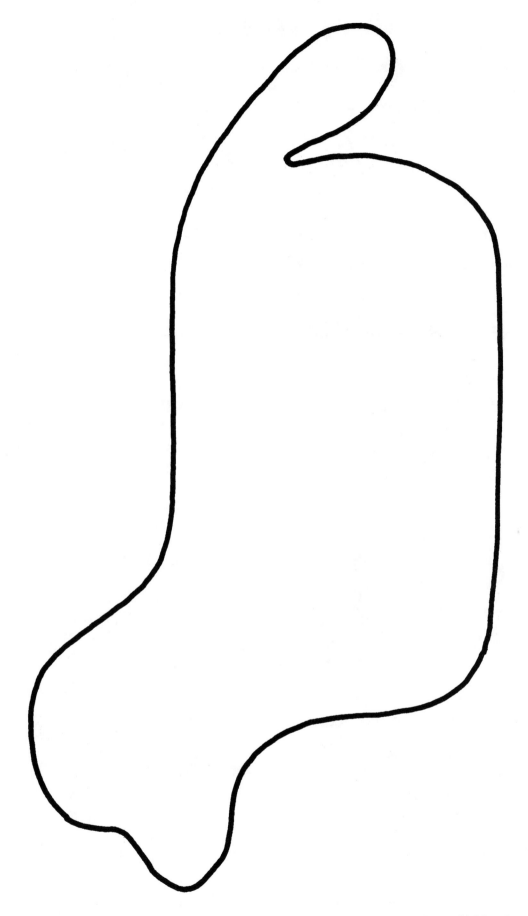

**Mary Had a Little Lamb    71**

# Mary, Mary, Quite Contrary

## Mary, Mary, Quite Contrary

Mary, Mary, quite contrary,
How does your garden grow?
With silver bells
And cockleshells,
And pretty maids all in a row.

*Traditional*

## Mary's Garden Mural

Place a long piece of butcher paper on a table or on the floor. Set out seed and flower catalogs. Have your children tear out pictures of flowers from the catalogs and glue them on the butcher paper to create a garden mural. Hang the completed mural on a wall or a bulletin board.

## Gardening in Rows

Let your children plant seeds in their own garden "rows." Remove the lids from several cardboard egg cartons and save for another use. Cut the bottoms of the egg cartons in half lengthwise to create rows. Give each child one row. Let the children fill the egg cups in their rows with potting soil. Then let them plant fast-growing seeds (sunflower, radish, marigold, etc.) in the dirt. From time to time, ask your children to tell how their gardens are growing.

## Flannelboard Fun

Photocopy the patterns on page 76 and cut them out. If desired, cover them with clear self-stick paper. Attach felt strips to the backs of the patterns. Place Mary on a flannelboard. As you recite the "Mary, Mary, Quite Contrary" rhyme, add rows of silver bells, cockleshells and pretty maids.

## We Are Flowers

For each of your children, make a paper-plate "flower" and color it red, yellow, orange, blue or pink. Add a green construction-paper stem. Have your children hold the flowers in their hands and sit in a circle. As you begin reading the following poem, have the children hunch over their flowers and pretend to be buds that have not opened yet. As you name each color of flower, have the children holding flowers of the same color uncurl themselves and stand up.

We are all such pretty flowers
Growing in Mary's garden bed.
When the rain comes down,
Up come the flowers of red.
  (Red flowers stand up.)

We are flowers that have grown
In the warmth of the sun.
Mary tends us gently,
Up come the yellow ones.
  (Yellow flowers stand up.)

We are flowers in the springtime,
We wear our petals bright.
Up come the orange flowers,
They are quite a pretty sight.
  (Orange flowers stand up.)

We are blossoms all in bloom,
Here are some in shades of blue.
  (Blue flowers stand up.)
And some of us are wearing pink
That glistens in the morning dew.
  (Pink flowers stand up.)

We are flowers in the garden,
We are Mary's pride and joy.
But if you look more closely,
You'll see we're girls and boys!

*Susan M. Paprocki*

## Flower Matching Game

Cut 15 flower shapes out of construction paper. Glue each flower shape to the top of a craft stick. Place playdough in the bottoms of five paper cups. "Plant" a different number of flowers from 1 to 5 in each cup. Number five index cards from 1 to 5. Set out the cups and the cards. Let your children take turns selecting a cup, counting the flowers in it and finding the matching numbered card.

## How Does Your Garden Grow?

Use one of the flower patterns on page 77 to cut flower shapes out of three or four different colors of felt. Place some of the flowers on a flannelboard in a pattern. Ask one of your children to use the remaining flowers to continue your pattern or to make the same one underneath yours.

*Variation*: Instead of using the same flower pattern and different colors of felt, use all four flower patterns on page 77 and the same color felt.

## Flowers Growing

Have your children curl up on the floor and pretend they are flower seeds planted in the dirt. Ask them to slowly uncurl and stand up as they start to grow. Have them fold their arms tightly across their chests like flower buds. Then have them slowly lift their arms above their heads to become flowers in bloom.

## Mary Planted Her Garden
Sung to: "Mary Had a Little Lamb"

Mary planted her garden,
Her garden, her garden.
Mary planted her garden
With rows of pretty bells.

Mary planted her garden,
Her garden, her garden.
Mary planted her garden
With rows of cockleshells.

Let your children make up additional verses as desired.

*Gayle Bittinger*

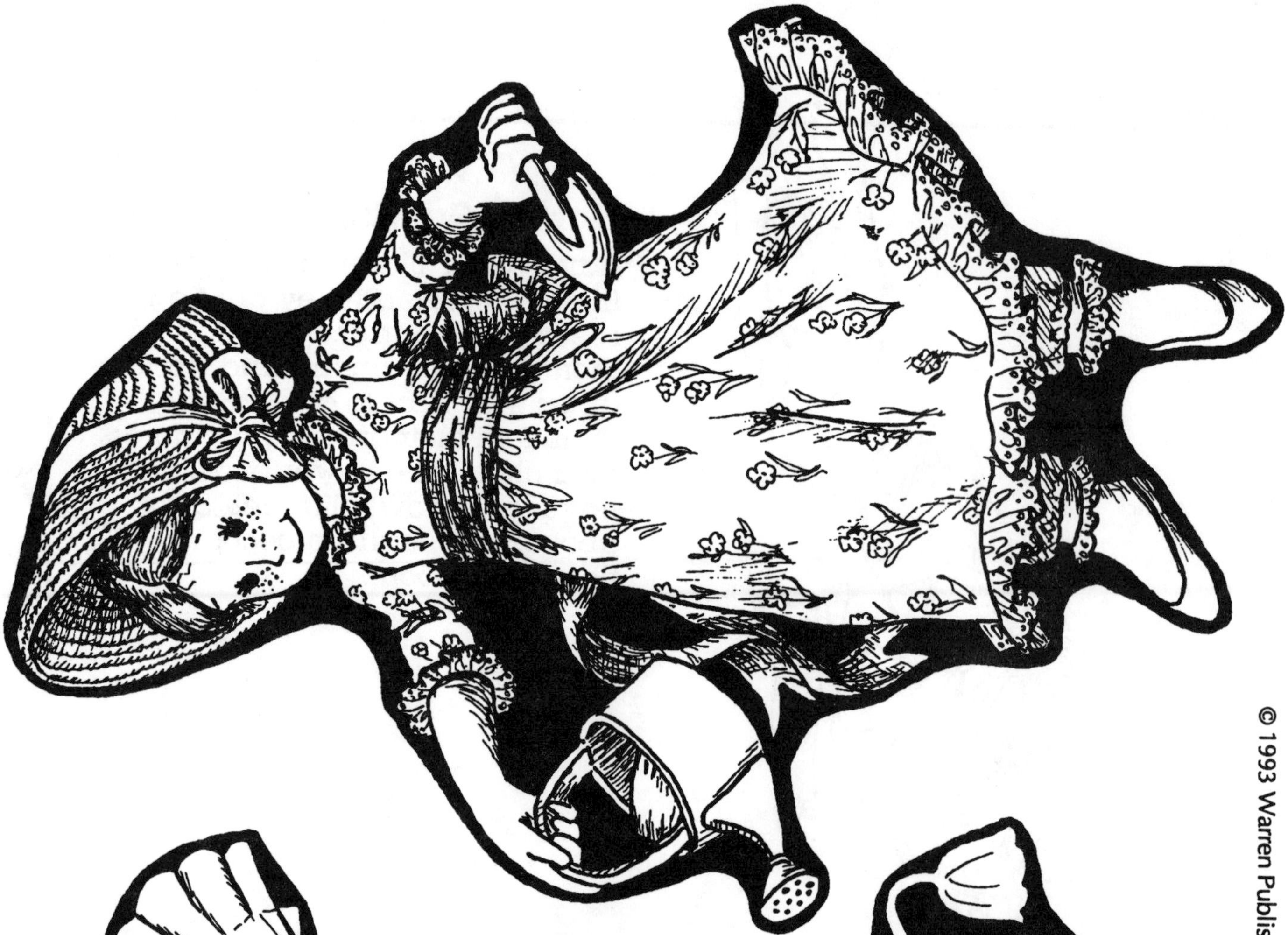

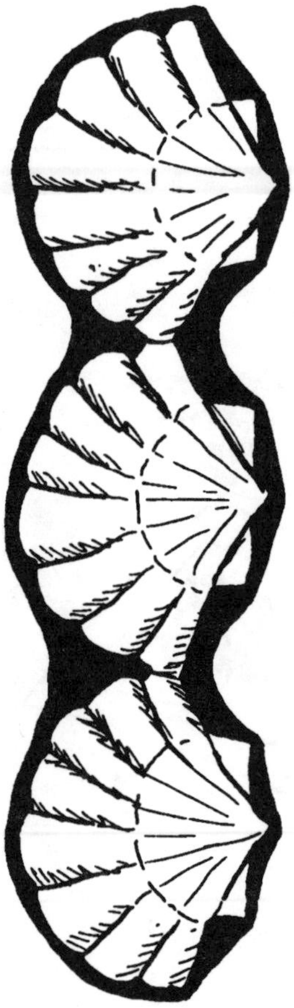

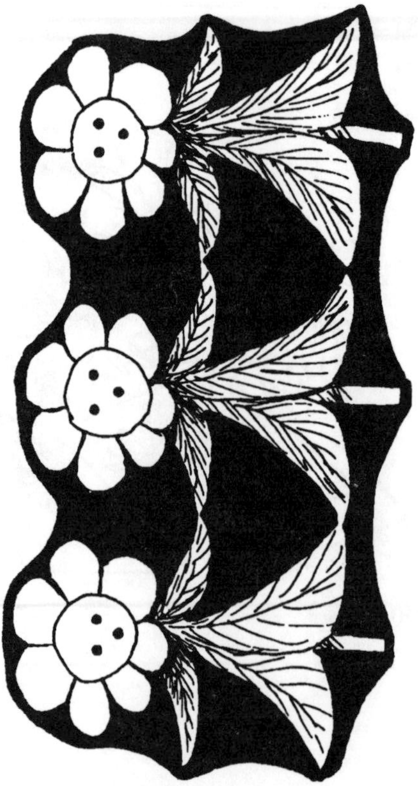

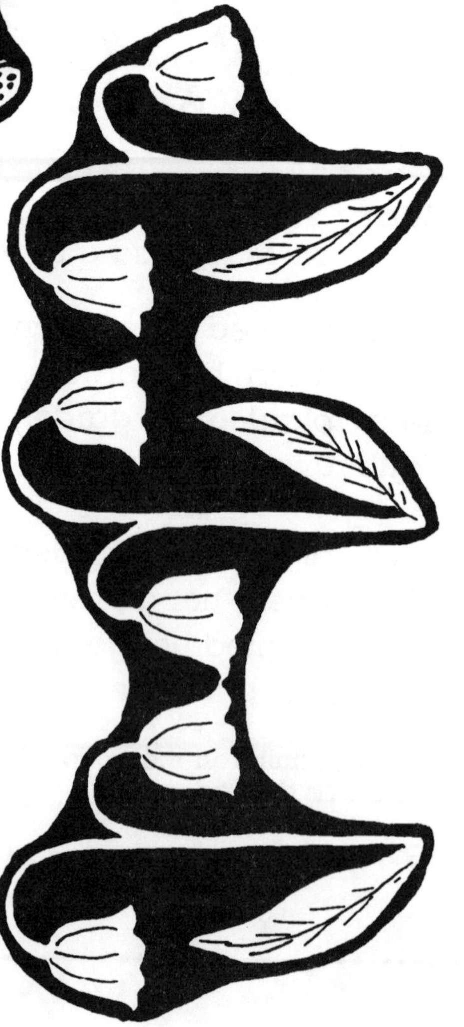

**Mary, Mary, Quite Contrary 77**

# The Muffin Man

## The Muffin Man

Oh, do you know the muffin man,
The muffin man, the muffin man?
Oh, do you know the muffin man
Who lives in Drury Lane?

Oh, yes, I know the muffin man,
The muffin man, the muffin man.
Oh, yes, I know the muffin man
Who lives in Drury Lane.

*Traditional*

## Blueberry Muffin Art

Cut muffin shapes out of light brown construction paper. Use a hole punch to punch circles out of blue construction paper. Give each child one of the muffin shapes and some blue circles. Have the children glue the circle "blueberries" to their muffin shapes to make blueberry muffins.

## What Did You Bake?

Read the following poem to your children, letting one of them tell you what kind of muffin was made. Repeat until each child has had a turn naming a kind of muffin.

Muffin Man, Muffin Man,
What did you make?
Muffin Man, Muffin Man,
What did you bake?

I made a _____ muffin,
Fluffy and light.
I made a _____ muffin,
Care for a bite?

*Jean Warren*

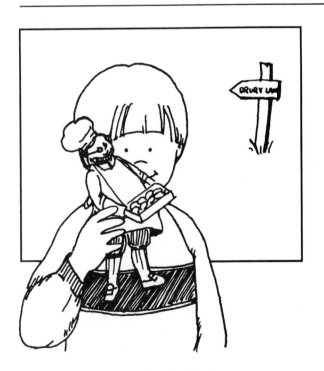

## Flannelboard Fun

Photocopy the patterns on page 83 and cut them out. If desired, cover them with clear self-stick paper. Attach strips of felt to the backs of the patterns. Place the patterns on a flannelboard as you recite or sing the rhyme "The Muffin Man" to your children.

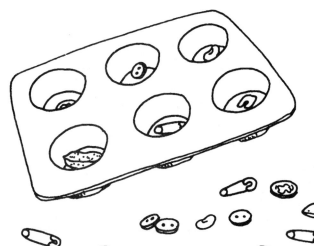

## Muffin Tin Sorting Game

Place a different kind of small object in each cup of a 6-cup muffin tin (a penny in one cup, a button in another cup, etc.). Give one of your children a box containing several of each object. Let the child sort the objects by placing them in the appropriate cups.

## Muffin Tin Color Game

Color the inside bottom of six paper baking cups a different color and place them in a 6-cup muffin tin. Cut small, matching colored circles out of construction paper. Let your children take turns placing each colored circle in the matching colored baking cup.

*Variation:* Instead of paper circles, let your children sort matching colored buttons or beads.

## Muffin Tin Counting Game

Number the inside bottoms of six paper baking cups from 1 to 6 and place them in a 6-cup muffin tin in random order. Set out 21 buttons, beads or pennies. Have one of your children put the appropriate number of items into each baking cup.

*Hint:* As your children's counting skills increase, use a 12-cup muffin tin.

## Bake Shop

Prepare a bake shop for your children. Make baker hats out of white paper bags. Set out play-dough, rolling pins, muffin tins, aprons, a bake shop sign, price signs on toothpicks, hot pads or oven mitts, cooling racks and anything else you want to put in your bake shop.

## Muffin Tin Toss

Put muffin tins on the floor. Give each of your children six buttons or lids from plastic gallon milk jugs. Let the children try tossing their buttons or lids into the muffin tin cups. Have them count how many buttons or lids landed in the cups of the muffin tin. Encourage them to try to beat their own scores.

## Muffin Recipe

1 cup all-purpose flour
1 tablespoon baking powder
½ teaspoon salt
¾ cup whole-wheat flour
1 egg
½ cup unsweetened apple-juice
 concentrate
¼ cup *each* vegetable oil and
 milk
1 banana, sliced

Sift all-purpose flour, baking powder and salt together. Stir in whole-wheat flour. Blend egg, apple-juice concentrate, oil, milk and banana in a blender. Combine dry and liquid ingredients. Spoon into greased or lined muffin tin cups. Bake at 400°F for 20 to 25 minutes. Makes 12 muffins.

**Fruit Muffins** — Add 1 cup chopped fresh or canned fruit to the mix before filling muffin tin cups. Peaches or blueberries are especially delicious.

**Bran Muffins** — Substitute 2 cups bran flakes for the whole-wheat flour.

**Surprise Muffins** — Partially fill the muffin cups with a little batter. Place a spoonful of applesauce or a little chopped fruit in each muffin cup. Then fill the muffin cups with the remaining batter.

## Muffins at Snacktime

Give your children the opportunity to try several different kinds of muffins, such as fruit muffins, corn muffins, plain muffins and English muffins. Make a different kind of muffin each day or serve three or four at one time and let them try a little of each kind.

**The Muffin Man    83**

# The Mulberry Bush

## The Mulberry Bush

Here we go round the mulberry bush,
The mulberry bush, the mulberry bush,
Here we go round the mulberry bush,
On a cold and frosty morning.

This is the way we wash our clothes,
Wash our clothes, wash our clothes,
This is the way we wash our clothes,
On a cold and frosty morning.

This is the way we wash our hands,
Wash our hands, wash our hands,
This is the way we wash our hands,
On a cold and frosty morning.

This is the way we go to school,
Go to school, go to school,
This is the way we go to school,
On a cold and frosty morning.

*Traditional*

## Health Mural

Recite or sing "The Mulberry Bush" with your children. Talk about the healthy habits mentioned in the rhyme. Then hang a long piece of butcher paper on a wall or a bulletin board at the children's eye level. Write "For Our Health" across the top of the paper. Let your children look through magazines to find pictures of people doing healthy things. Have the children tear out the pictures and attach them to the mural. Encourage them to talk about what is happening in the pictures and why those are good things to do.

## Color Rhyme

Read the following poem to your children. Encourage them to fill in the rhyming color word at the end of each verse.

What will I wear to school today,
Something old or something new?
What will I wear to school today?
Perhaps the color blue.

What will I wear to school today,
Something that covers my head?
What will I wear to school today?
Perhaps the color red.

What will I wear to school today,
Something happy or something
  mean?
What will I wear to school today?
Perhaps the color green.

What will I wear to school today,
Something wild or something
  mellow?
What will I wear to school today?
Perhaps the color yellow.

What will I wear to school today,
Something dull or something bright?
What will I wear to school today?
Perhaps the color white.

What will I wear to school today,
Something with hearts or with
  a clown?
What will I wear to school today?
Perhaps the color brown.

What will I wear to school today,
Something that buttons in front
  or in back?
What will I wear to school today?
Perhaps the color black.

*Jean Warren*

## Flannelboard Fun

Photocopy the pattern cards on page 88 and cut them out. If desired, cover them with clear self-stick paper. Attach strips of felt to the backs of the cards. Recite the rhyme "The Mulberry Bush" with your children, placing the cards on a flannelboard one at a time.

## Morning Routines

Photocopy the pattern cards on pages 88 and 89 and cut them out. If desired, cover the cards with clear self-stick paper. Show the cards to your children. Ask them to tell you what is happening in each picture. Then let your children take turns selecting cards that show the things they do in the morning and arranging them in the appropriate order.

*Extension:* Have your children act out their morning routines after telling about them.

## Good Health Game

Place on a tray a variety of good health items such as a comb, brush, washcloth, bar of soap, facial tissue, jump rope and apple. Have your children sit in a circle. Ask them how they feel when they are healthy and how they feel when they are not. Then let each child in turn select an item from the tray, tell how it helps him or her stay healthy and place the item in the middle of the circle.

## Healthy Habits
Sung to: "Row, Row, Row Your Boat"

Eat, eat, from all food groups
To keep your body strong.
Too much candy, junk and pop
Does your body wrong.

Rest, rest, get good rest
Each and every night.
Feel perky in the morning
When your nighttime's right.

Wash, wash, both your hands
Use a lot of soap.
Don't give cold and flu germs
Any kind of hope.

*Susan M. Paprocki*

**88** **The Mulberry Bush**

**The Mulberry Bush  89**

# Old Mother Hubbard

### Old Mother Hubbard

Old Mother Hubbard
Went to the cupboard,
To fetch her poor dog a bone;
But when she got there
The cupboard was bare
And so the poor dog had none.

*Traditional*

### Old-Mother-Hubbard Cupboards

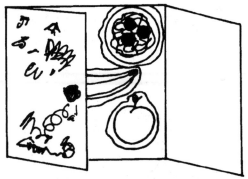

Old Mother Hubbard needs to fill her cupboard. Lay a piece of construction paper horizontally and fold the two sides into the middle (as shown in the illustration) to make a cupboard. Give one to each child. Have your children decorate the cupboard doors as desired. Then let them tear pictures of foods out of magazines. Have them open the doors of the cupboards and glue the food pictures inside.

### Flannelboard Fun

Photocopy the Mother Hubbard, dog and cupboard patterns on pages 94 and 95. Cut out the patterns, being sure to cut along the dotted lines of the cupboard pattern to make doors. If desired, cover the patterns with clear self-stick paper. Attach strips of felt to the backs of the patterns. Place the patterns on a flannelboard. Recite the rhyme "Old Mother Hubbard" to your children, opening the doors of the cupboard at the end of the rhyme to reveal the empty cupboard.

## Counting Rhyme

Use the dog bone pattern on
page 95 as a guide for cutting
four dog bone shapes out of felt.
As you recite the following rhyme,
add one bone at a time to a
flannelboard.

Old Mother Hubbard went to the cupboard
To fetch her poor dog a bone;
But when she got there the cupboard was bare
And so the poor dog had none.

Old Mother Hubbard went to the butcher
To get a bone, all alone;
When she got home she put in the bone
And now her cupboard has one.

Old Mother Hubbard went to the butcher
For another bone, it's true;
When she got home she put in the bone
And now her cupboard has two.

Old Mother Hubbard went to the butcher
To get another, you see;
When she got home she put in the bone
And now her cupboard has three.

Old Mother Hubbard went to the butcher
And asked for just one more;
When she got home she put in the bone
And now her cupboard has four.

*Jean Warren*

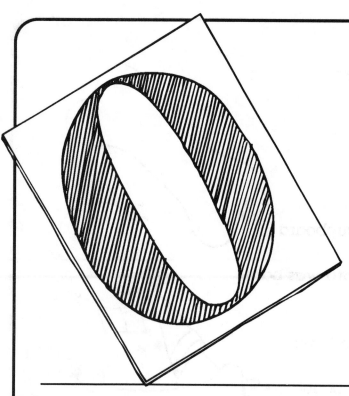

## Counting Zero

Ask your children to count objects around the room, as you name them. Call out a few objects of which there are none. For example, have the children tell you that there are zero crocodiles, fire engines, moons, etc., in the room. Then write the numeral 0 where the children can see it.

## Dog Tricks

Have the children pretend to be dogs by crawling around on all fours. Encourage them to romp around and play like dogs and puppies. Let one of the children pretend to be the trainer and ask the others to do doggy tricks such as sit up, roll over, fetch (with their paws, instead of their mouths), and beg.

## No Bones Were in the Cupboard
Sung to: "The Farmer in the Dell"

No bones were in the cupboard,
No bones were in the cupboard.
The cupboard was bare,
No bones in there,
No bones were in the cupboard.

The dog found one outside,
The dog found one outside,
He had none
Till he found one,
The dog found one outside.

Let your children name other places the dog could find a bone. Repeat the song, substituting the name of one of those places for *outside*.

*Gayle Bittinger*

## Doggy Bone Snacks

Spread slices of toast or bread with peanut butter. Cut the slices into bone shapes with a knife or a cookie cutter. Serve the "doggy bone" snacks to your children.

**94** **Old Mother Hubbard**

**Old Mother Hubbard    95**

# One, Two, Buckle My Shoe

### One, Two, Buckle My Shoe

One, two,
Buckle my shoe;
Three, four,
Shut the door;
Five, six,
Pick up sticks;
Seven, eight,
Lay them straight;
Nine, ten,
A big red hen.

*Traditional*

### Shoe Art Show

Help each child trace around his or her shoe on a piece of construction paper. Then let your children use crayons to turn their shoe tracings into funny pictures. When they are finished, display their papers on a wall or a bulletin board and have a "Shoe Art Show."

## Flannelboard Fun

Photocopy the patterns on pages 100 and 101 and cut them out. If desired, cover them with clear self-stick paper. Attach felt strips to the backs of the patterns. As you read the rhyme "One, Two, Buckle My Shoe" to your children, place the patterns on a flannelboard in order: the shoe, the door, the sticks in a pile, the sticks laid straight and, finally, the hen.

## Number Books

Give each of your children 10 pieces of construction paper numbered from 1 to 10. Set out magazine pictures and glue. Have your children glue the corresponding number of pictures to each page. As each child finishes, add a cover to his or her pages and staple them together. Write "My Number Book" on each child's cover, along with the child's name. Encourage your children to read their books to you and to one another by naming and counting the items on each page.

## Sequence Cards

Draw simple pictures of a shoe, a door, sticks in a pile, sticks laid straight and a hen on separate index cards. Mix up the cards. Let your children take turns putting them in the order in which they are mentioned in the rhyme "One, Two, Buckle My Shoe". If necessary, recite the rhyme as they put the cards in sequence.

## Let's Find Our Shoes

Have each of your children give you one of his or her shoes. While the children wait out of sight, hide the shoes around the room. When you are ready, call out "One, two, buckle your shoe!" Let the children look for their shoes. Encourage them to cooperate and help one another find and put on their shoes. When they are done, have them sit down. If desired, let the children race against the clock as they play this game, trying to improve their score each time they play.

## Coordination Stations

Set up coordination stations to go along with the activities in the rhyme "One, Two, Buckle My Shoe." At the first station, set out a pair of shoes for your children to buckle and unbuckle. Put a playhouse with a door to open and shut at the second station. At the third station, place a pile of sticks for the children to pick up and lay straight. Finally, at the fourth station, set out a picture of a hen and have the children pretend to be hens pecking all around the ground.

## Before I Go to Market Today
Sung to: "The Muffin Man"

Before I go to market today,
Market today, market today,
Before I go to market today,
I'll buckle up my shoes.

Before I go to market today,
Market today, market today,
Before I go to market today,
I'll shut the big barn door.

Before I go to market today,
Market today, market today,
Before I go to market today,
I'll gather up kindling sticks.

Before I go to market today,
Market today, market today,
Before I go to market today,
I'll stack my sticks up straight.

Before I go to market today,
Market today, market today,
Before I go to market today,
I'll feed my big red hen.

*Jean Warren*

## Counting Snacks

For each of your children, cut off the last two egg cups of an egg carton to make a carton with 10 egg-cup sections. In each egg cup place a different number of snack foods (from 1 to 10); for example, one piece of cheese, two crackers, three orange segments, four pretzels, five grapes, six carrot sticks, seven olive slices, eight shelled peanuts, nine pieces of O-shaped cereal and ten raisins.

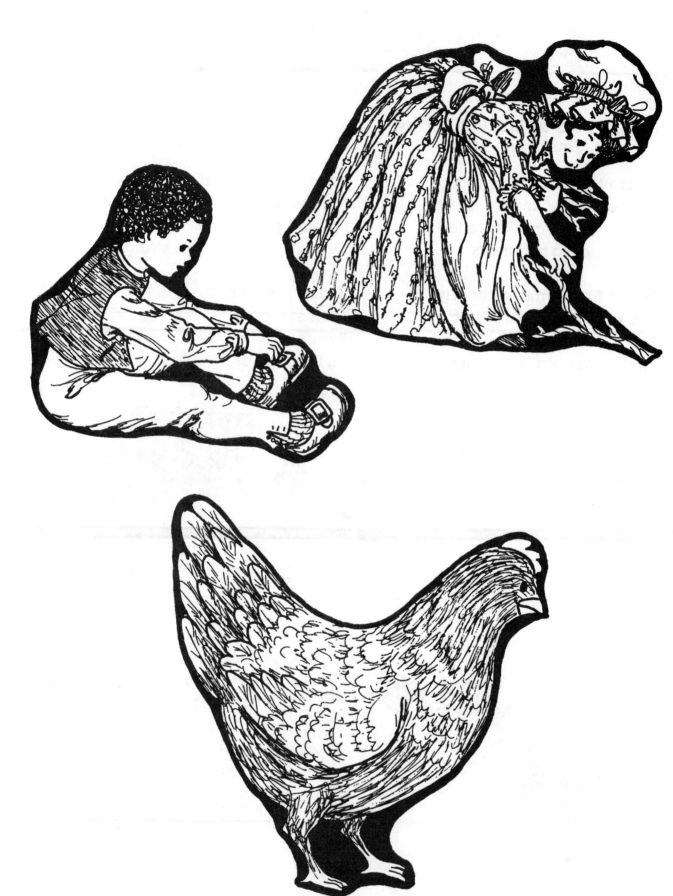

**100   One, Two, Buckle My Shoe**

# Pease Porridge Hot

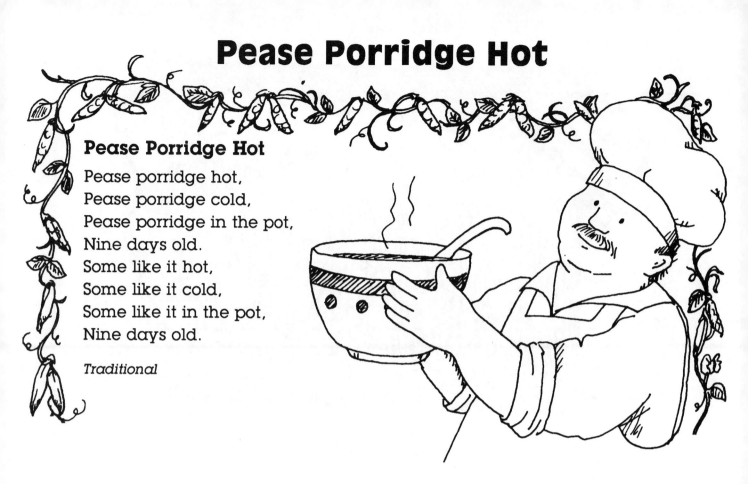

## Pease Porridge Hot

Pease porridge hot,
Pease porridge cold,
Pease porridge in the pot,
Nine days old.
Some like it hot,
Some like it cold,
Some like it in the pot,
Nine days old.

*Traditional*

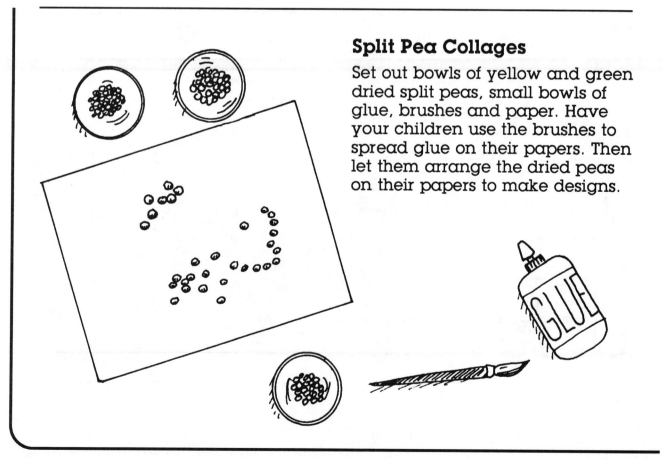

## Split Pea Collages

Set out bowls of yellow and green dried split peas, small bowls of glue, brushes and paper. Have your children use the brushes to spread glue on their papers. Then let them arrange the dried peas on their papers to make designs.

## Hot and Cold

Fill one bowl with ice water and another bowl with hot water. Show your children two thermometers that are at room temperature. Have the children observe that the liquid inside the thermometer, the mercury, is at the same point on each thermometer. Then put a thermometer in each bowl. Now ask the children to observe the difference between the thermometers. Tell them that heat makes the mercury rise while cold makes it fall. Ask the children to guess what would happen if the thermometers were taken out of the bowls.

## Flannelboard Fun

Photocopy the patterns on page 107 and cut them out. If desired, cover them with clear self-stick paper. Attach strips of felt to the backs of the patterns. As you recite the "Pease Porridge Hot" rhyme, place each pattern as it is named on a flannelboard. Ask your children to take turns pointing to the pease porridge they like best.

## Nesting Pots

Set out several cooking pots that can be stacked one inside the other. Ask your children to arrange the pots from largest to smallest. Then show them how to nest the pots, one inside the other, by starting with the largest pot.

## Sensory Exploration

Fill dishpans or a water-sensory table with dried split peas. Set out different sizes of cups, spoons, funnels and other utensils. Let your children explore this new sensory experience with their hands and the tools provided.

## One Little Pea

Have your children stand in a circle. As you recite the first verse of the following rhyme, select one child to pretend to be a pea and jump into the pretend pot in the middle of the circle and sit down. Continue with additional verses as needed until every child is in the pot. When all of the children are in the pot, recite the last verse and have them all jump out of the pot.

One little pea jumped into the pot,
And waited for the soup to get hot.

A second little pea jumped into the pot,
And waited for the soup to get hot.

Finally, the soup got so hot,
All the little peas jumped out of the pot!

*Jean Warren*

## This Is the Way
Sung to: "The Mulberry Bush"

This is the way we make pea soup,
Make pea soup, make pea soup.
This is the way we make pea soup
So early in the morning.

*Additional verses:* This is the way we wash the peas; cook the peas; add the milk; eat it up.

*Jean Warren*

## Simple Pease Porridge

1 can (10¾ ounces) condensed
green pea soup
1 cup chicken broth
½ cup water
1 cup diced, cooked potato
1 cup frozen peas, thawed

Blend ingredients in a blender.
Heat for 10 minutes and serve.

## Homemade Pease Porridge

2 cups dried peas
3 quarts water
1 ham bone
1 cup *each* minced onion and
chopped celery
2 cups chopped carrots

Rinse dried peas and place them in
a large sauce pan with water. Add
ham bone, onion, celery and carrots. Bring to a boil, then simmer
for 2 hours. Take out ham bone
and puree the remainder of the
soup in a blender. Remove ham
from bone and dice. Add to pureed
soup. Makes 16 small servings.

*Hint:* Give each of your children a
small cup of warm soup and a
small cup of cold soup. Let them
decide whether they like pease
porridge hot or pease porridge cold!

## Rhythm Clapping

Have your children listen carefully while you recite the rhyme
"Pease Porridge Hot" and clap on
each syllable. Recite the rhyme
again slowly and have the children clap along with you.

*Variation:* Instead of clapping on
each beat, have your children
clap only when they hear cer-
tain words such as hot and cold
or pease.

**Pease Porridge Hot 107**

# Peter, Peter, Pumpkin Eater

## Peter, Peter, Pumpkin Eater

Peter, Peter, pumpkin eater,
Had a mouse but couldn't keep her;
He put her in a pumpkin shell,
And there he kept her very well.

*Adapted Traditional*

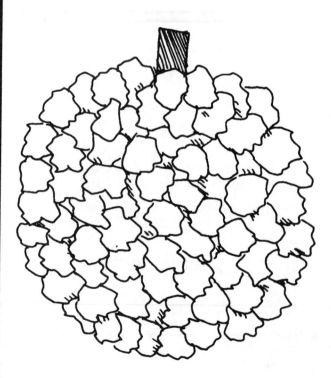

## Torn Paper Pumpkins

Give each of your children a small paper plate and a piece of orange construction paper. Let the children tear their orange papers into small pieces and glue the pieces all over their paper plates. Then let them glue on green construction-paper stems to complete their pumpkins.

*Extension:* Hang a long piece of butcher paper on a wall at the children's eye level. Attach the pumpkins to the butcher paper. Add vines and leaves with a green felt-tip marker to create a pumpkin patch mural.

## Pumpkin Observations

If possible, take your children on a field trip to a pumpkin farm. Let them choose a pumpkin to bring back to the room. Or bring in a pumpkin yourself for doing the following activities.

- Let your children touch and examine the pumpkin. Ask them to describe how it looks and feels. Then help them place the pumpkin on a scale to see how much it weighs.

- Cut off the top of the pumpkin and let the children observe the pulp and seeds inside. Ask them to estimate how many seeds there are. Scoop out the seeds and count them with the group. Were any estimates too high? Too low? Just right?

- Let each of your children cut off a length of yarn that he or she thinks will fit around the pumpkin. Have the child try wrapping the yarn piece around the pumpkin to see how well it fits. Measure and cut off a piece of yarn that fits around the pumpkin exactly. Let each child compare his or her yarn piece to the one that fits. Ask each child: "Is your yarn piece shorter or longer?"

## Where Are the Mice?

Select one child to be Peter. Have the rest of your children pretend to be Mice. Ask Peter to leave the room while the Mice scurry around and find places to hide in the room. Then have Peter come back into the room and try to find the Mice. As each Mouse is found, have him or her join the search for the remaining hidden Mice. When all of the Mice have been found, select a new Peter and begin the game again.

## Flannelboard Fun

Photocopy the patterns on page 112 and cut them out. If desired, cover them with clear self-stick paper. Attach felt strips to the backs of the patterns. Use the patterns on page 113 as guides for cutting a pumpkin shape and a pumpkin-top shape out of orange felt. Be sure to cut along the dotted line to make a window in the pumpkin shape. Place Peter, the mouse and the pumpkin shapes on a flannelboard. Recite the rhyme "Peter, Peter, Pumpkin Eater" to your children. When you come to the line "He put her in a pumpkin shell," have one of your children lift up the pumpkin top and place the mouse "inside" the pumpkin.

## Pumpkin Matching Cards

Draw identical jack-o'-lantern faces on a pair of index cards. Make several different pairs. Mix up the cards and give them to your children. Let the children take turns finding the matching pumpkin faces.

## Peter, Peter, Pumpkin Head
Sung to: "Twinkle, Twinkle, Little Star"

Peter, Peter, pumpkin head,
Eats pumpkin pies and pumpkin bread,
Pumpkin muffins, pumpkin cake,
And pumpkin cookies freshly baked.
Peter, Peter, pumpkin head,
Full of pumpkins, you're well fed.

*Diane Thom*

## Pumpkin Cookies

½ cup unsalted butter
1 teaspoon vanilla
1 can (6 ounces) unsweetened
    pineapple-juice concentrate
2 eggs
1½ cups cooked pumpkin
1 teaspoon cinnamon
4½ teaspoons baking powder
½ teaspoon nutmeg
2½ cups whole-wheat flour
1 cup *each* raisins and
    chopped nuts

Whip together butter, vanilla and pineapple-juice concentrate. Add eggs and cooked pumpkin. Mix in cinnamon, baking powder, nutmeg and whole-wheat flour. Stir in raisins and chopped nuts.

Cover a cookie sheet with aluminum foil and grease it. Drop teaspoonfuls of the dough onto the foil. Bake at 375°F for 15 minutes or until browned.

**112    Peter, Peter, Pumpkin Eater**

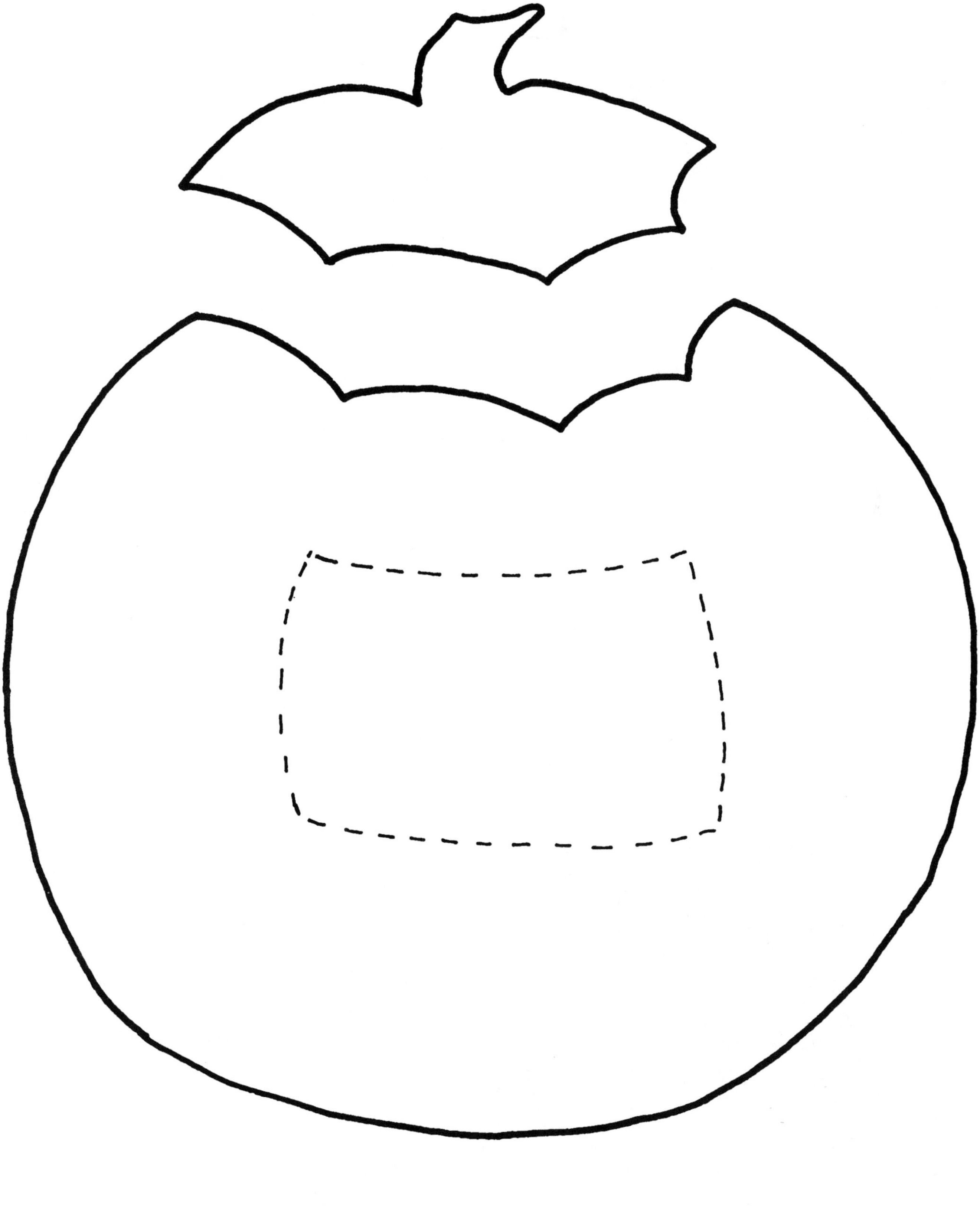

# The Queen of Hearts

## The Queen of Hearts

The Queen of Hearts,
She made some tarts,
All on a summer's day;
The Knave of Hearts,
He stole the tarts,
And with them ran away.

The King of Hearts
Called for the tarts,
And scolded the Knave full score;
The Knave of Hearts
Brought back the tarts,
And vowed he'd steal no more.

*Adapted Traditional*

## Heart Crowns

Give each child a construction-paper crown shape and a variety of heart stickers. Let the children decorate their crowns with the stickers. Then have them wrap their crowns around their heads while you tape them in place. Let your children wear their crowns while they pretend to be the Kings and Queens of Hearts.

*Variation:* Instead of decorating the crowns with heart stickers, let your children decorate them with glued-on construction-paper heart shapes.

## Heart Prints

Have your children brush white vinegar on white construction paper. Then let them cover their papers with precut red tissue-paper heart shapes. As the vinegar dries, the tissue paper will fall off, leaving red heart prints.

## Mirror Hearts

Cut small heart shapes from red or pink construction paper. Then cut the hearts in half. Give each child a hand mirror and half of a paper heart. Have the children place their heart halves on a table. Let them experiment with standing their hand mirrors next to their heart halves to make the half-hearts appear to be whole hearts.

## Flannelboard Fun

Photocopy the patterns on pages 118 and 119 and cut them out. If desired, cover them with clear self-stick paper. Attach strips of felt to the backs of the patterns. Place the patterns on a flannelboard. Recite the rhyme "The Queen of Hearts" to your children, moving the patterns accordingly. Then let your children use the patterns to retell the rhyme.

## Rhyming Hearts

Cut heart shapes out of red construction paper. Glue a magazine picture of an object on each one. Place the hearts in a paper bag. Let a child draw a heart out of the bag and name the object pictured on it. Then have the rest of your children think of words that rhyme with the object's name. Continue until each child has had a chance to draw a heart out of the bag.

## Heart Hunt

Cut heart shapes out of construction paper. Hide the hearts around your room. Then let your children have a Heart Hunt. The child who finds the most hearts gets to be the King or Queen of Hearts for the day. Be sure that every child finds a few hearts.

## Knave of Hearts

This game is similar to musical chairs. Give each of your children a paper heart. Have the children place their hearts on a table (or the floor) in the middle of the room. Have the children walk around the table while you play some music. While the music plays, the Knave of Hearts (you or another child) sneaks in and steals one of the hearts. When the music stops, each child tries to grab a heart. The child who does not get a heart leaves the game and becomes the next Knave. The last one or two children in the game are the winners. Be sure that everyone has a paper heart at the end of the game.

## Queen of Hearts Tarts

½ cup *each* margarine and
    cottage cheese
1 cup all-purpose flour
1 tablespoon cinnamon

Cream margarine and cottage cheese together. Add flour and cinnamon. Roll the dough into small balls, adding more flour if sticky. Divide dough into 12 balls. Turn two 6-cup muffin tins upside down and grease the bottoms. Place a dough ball on each up-side-down muffin cup and mold it around the cup to form a small tart shell. Bake at 350°F for 25 to 30 minutes. Cool and remove. Fill tart shells with Strawberry Cream Filling (below).

### Strawberry Cream Filling —
Thaw unsweetened frozen straw-berries. Dice the strawberries into small pieces and whip them with softened cream cheese and chopped walnuts.

**118    The Queen of Hearts**

**The Queen of Hearts   119**

# Rabbit, Rabbit, Carrot Eater

### Rabbit, Rabbit, Carrot Eater

Rabbit, rabbit, carrot eater,
He says there is nothing sweeter,
Than a carrot every day,
Munch and crunch and run away.

*Traditional*

## Foot-Shaped Rabbits

Trace around each child's foot on a piece of white construction paper. Let your children cut out their foot shapes (or cut them out yourself). Then let the children turn their shapes into side-view rabbits. Show each child how to position his or her shape horizontally so that the narrow end forms the rabbit's head and the wider part forms the rabbit's body. Give the children construction paper ears, facial features, whiskers, feet and inner-ear shapes to glue on as shown in the illustration. Then have the children glue on cotton balls for tails.

## Carrot Gardens

Cut off and save the top 2 inches of an extra-thick carrot. Hollow out the middle of the carrot as shown. Make three small holes near the cut end of the carrot and attach strings for hanging. Make one for each child or group of children. Have your children fill the holes in their carrots with potting soil. Then give them cress or mustard seed to plant in the dirt. Hang the carrot gardens in a sunny place. Have the children check their gardens daily and water them to keep the soil moist.

## Flannelboard Fun

Photocopy the patterns on page 124 and cut them out. If desired, cover them with clear self-stick paper. Attach strips of felt to the backs of the patterns. Place the rabbit and carrot on a flannelboard as you recite the rhyme "Rabbit, Rabbit, Carrot Eater" to your children.

## Out in the Garden

Cut 15 carrot shapes out of felt. Place all of the carrots on a flannel-board. Substitute the names of your children for the names in the following poem. As you say a child's name, have that child take the appropriate number of carrots off the flannelboard, one at a time, as you count out loud.

*Variation*: Instead of felt carrot shapes, "plant" 15 real carrots (with tops attached) in a box of dirt.

Out in the garden
Under the sun,
Grew some carrots,
Ryan picked one.
 (One.)

Out in the garden
Under skies so blue,
Grew some carrots,
Katie picked two.
 (One, two.)

Out in the garden
Near a big oak tree,
Grew some carrots,
Chris picked three.
 (One, two, three.)

Out in the garden
By the back door,
Grew some carrots,
Andrew picked four.
 (One, two, three, four.)

Out in the garden
Near a beehive,
Grew some carrots,
Emily picked five.
 (One, two, three, four, five.)

We took those carrots
And washed the whole bunch,
Then we all sat down
And ate them for lunch.
 (Munch, munch, munch, munch, munch.)

*Jean Warren*

## Vegetable Lotto Game

Make two photocopies of the Vegetable Lotto Game board on page 125. Glue each one to a piece of posterboard. Cut one game board into cards. Cover the cards and remaining game board with clear self-stick paper for durability, if desired. Let your children take turns placing the game cards on top of the matching pictures on the game board.

## Down by the Garden
Sung to: "Down by the Station"

Down by the garden
Early in the morning,
See the little carrots all in a row.
See the hungry rabbit
Pulling up the carrots.
Munch, munch, crunch, crunch,
Off he goes.

*Jean Warren*

## Sweet Carrot Sticks

Cut carrots into sticks. Place in a container and pour in unsweetened pineapple juice to cover. Chill for at least one hour before serving.

**124    Rabbit, Rabbit, Carrot Eater**

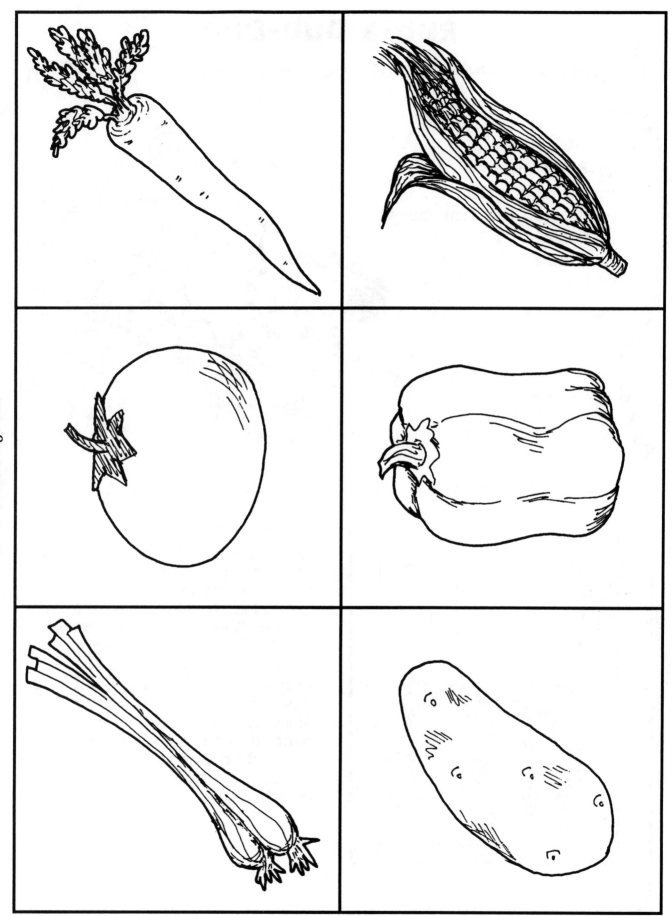

**Rabbit, Rabbit, Carrot Eater     125**

# Rub-a-Dub-Dub

## Rub-a-Dub-Dub

Rub-a-dub-dub,
Three men in a tub,
And who do you think they be?
The butcher, the baker,
The candlestick maker,
Helpers they are, all three.

*Adapted Traditional*

## Three Men in a Tub Art

Have each child place one hand in the middle of a piece of light-blue construction paper. Trace around each child's three middle fingers. Give each child a brown construction-paper tub shape. Have the children glue their tub shapes below their finger out-lines. Then have them use cray-ons to add wavy ocean lines beneath the tub. Help your chil-dren add a face to each of their finger outlines to make "three men in a tub."

## Sink or Float

Fill a dishpan with water. Place a small plastic container in the dishpan. Set out several objects of various weights. Let your children experiment to find out which objects they can put into the container without sinking it.

## Flannelboard Fun

Photocopy the pattern on page 131 and cut it out. If desired, cover it with clear self-stick paper. Attach felt strips to the back of the pattern. Place the pattern on a flannel-board. Recite the rhyme "Rub-a-Dub-Dub" to your children, pointing out each character as he is named.

## Community Helpers

After your children are familiar with the "Rub-a-Dub-Dub" rhyme, have them substitute the names of other helpers for the butcher, the baker and the candlestick maker. Talk with your children about what each of the helpers does.

## Occupational Charades

Provide your children with a box of hats worn by different kinds of helpers, such as bakers, construction workers, firefighters, baseball players, clowns, etc. Let them take turns selecting a hat from the box and acting out what a person who wears that kind of hat does.

## Learning in Threes

Collect an assortment of objects in sets of three such as three wooden spoons, three measuring cups, three balls, three toy cars, etc. Mix up the objects and let your children take turns finding the sets of three.

## Row Your Boat

Divide your children into pairs and have them sit on the floor. Have the children in each pair face each other, touch their feet together and hold hands. Show your children how to alternate bending forward and backward, as if they were rowing. Ask them to row slowly and then gradually row faster and faster. Sing the following song while your children row.

Sung to: "Row, Row, Row Your Boat"

Row, row, row our boats,
Gently down the stream,
The more we row, the farther we go,
Watch us while we row.

*Jean Warren*

## Little Helpers
Sung to: "Ten Little Indians"

One little, two little, three little helpers,
Four little, five little, six little helpers,
Seven little, eight little, nine little helpers,
Working hard today.

*Jean Warren*

## Helpers They Are, All Three
Sung to: "The Farmer in the Dell"

The butcher cuts the meat,
The butcher cuts the meat,
He cuts the steak for us to eat,
The butcher cuts the meat.

The baker bakes the bread,
The baker bakes the bread,
Bagels, rolls and biscuits too,
The baker bakes the bread.

The candlestick maker,
The candlestick maker,
Dips candles to light the night,
The candlestick maker.

*Bobbie Lee Wagman*

# Three Little Kittens

## Three Little Kittens

Three little kittens
They lost their mittens,
And they began to cry,
"Oh, Mother dear,
We sadly fear
Our mittens we have lost!"

"What! Lost your mittens,
You naughty kittens.
Then you shall have no pie."

"Meow, meow, meow!"

The three little kittens
Found their mittens,
And they began to cry,
"Oh, Mother dear,
See here, see here,
Our mittens we have found."

"What! Found your mittens,
You good little kittens!
Then you shall have some pie."

"Purr, purr, purr."

*Traditional*

## Mitten Collages

Use the large mitten pattern on page 137 to cut mitten shapes out of wallpaper sample pages and various colors of construction paper. Hide the mitten shapes around the room. Have your children "find" all the mittens. Then give them large pieces of construction paper. Let them glue all the mittens they found on their papers to make mitten collages.

## Mitten Puppets

Give each of your children a mitten. Let the children turn their mittens into puppets by gluing on sequins, buttons, yarn, rickrack, ribbon and fabric scraps. Encourage them to use their puppets to talk to friends, tell stories or sing songs.

## Happy and Sad Puppets

Give each of your children a paper plate. Have the children draw happy faces on the fronts of their plates and sad faces on the backs. Attach craft-stick handles to the plates to complete the puppets. Read the rhyme "Three Little Kittens" to your children. When the kittens loose their mittens, have your children hold up the sad faces of their puppets and cry "Boo-hoo." When the kittens find their mittens, have your children hold up the happy faces and shout "Hurray!"

## Flannelboard Fun

Photocopy the mother cat pattern on page 136. Make three photocopies of each of the kitten and small mitten patterns on page 137. Cut out the patterns. If desired, cover them with clear self-stick paper. Attach strips of felt to the backs of the patterns. Place the mother cat and the three kittens on a flannelboard. Recite the first two verses of the "Three Little Kittens" rhyme to your children. Add the mitten shapes to the flannelboard, then recite the last two verses.

## Mitten Pairs

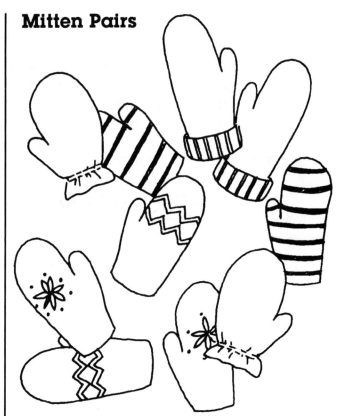

Collect pairs of different colored mittens. Mix up the pairs and put them in a pile. Let your children find the matching pairs of mittens.

## Matching Game

Cut one kitten shape with paws extended (see illustration) and two mitten shapes out of the same color of felt. Repeat, using several other colors of felt. Place the kitten shapes on a flannelboard and set out the mitten shapes. Let your children take turns selecting a pair of mittens and placing them on the paws of the matching colored kitten.

## Three Little Kittens
Sung to: "Ten Little Indians"

Three little kittens lost their mittens,
Three little kittens lost their mittens,
Three little kittens lost their mittens,
Now they'll have no pie.

Three little kittens found their mittens,
Three little kittens found their mittens,
Three little kittens found their mittens,
Now they'll have some pie.

*Gayle Bittinger*

## Sweet Potato Pie

¼ cup unsweetened apple-juice
   concentrate
2 cups cooked sweet potatoes
⅓ cup unsweetened orange juice
1 banana, sliced
1 teaspoon cinnamon
2 eggs
Single pie crust

Blend apple-juice concentrate,
sweet potatoes, orange juice,
banana, cinnamon and eggs in a
blender. Pour the mixture into pie
crust and bake at 350°F for 40
minutes.

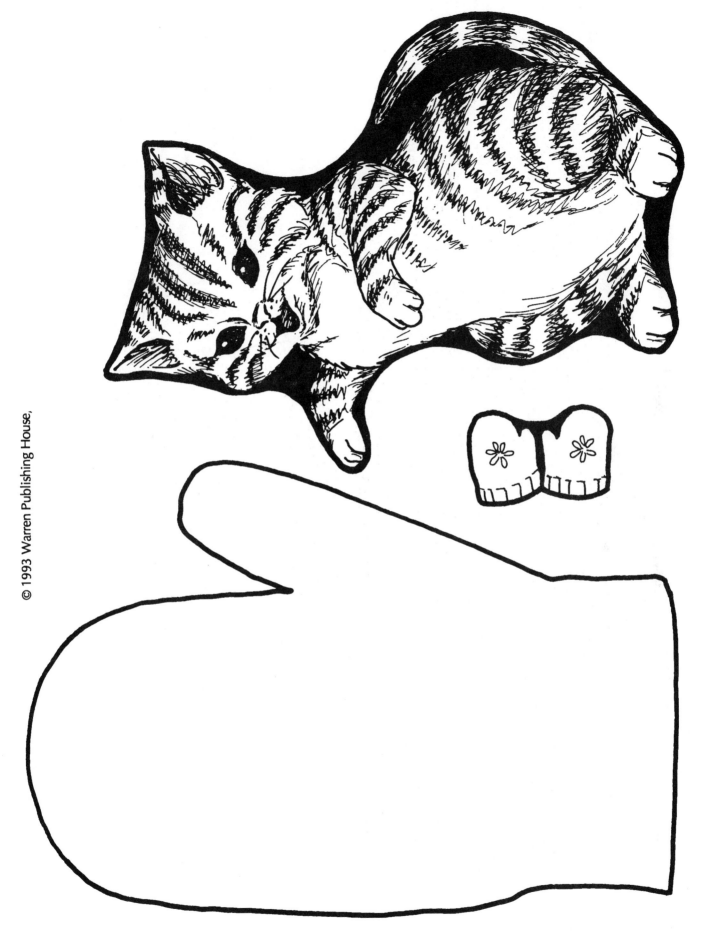

**Three Little Kittens   137**

# Twinkle, Twinkle, Little Star

### Twinkle, Twinkle, Little Star

Twinkle, twinkle, little star,
How I wonder what you are!
Up above the world so high,
Like a diamond in the sky.

*Traditional*

### Star Printing

Set out star-shaped cookie cutters, potato halves with stars cut out, or star shapes cut out of plastic foam trays. Make paint pads by folding paper towels in half, placing them in shallow containers and pouring on small amounts of tempera paint. Let your children use the stamping materials to make star prints on pieces of construction paper.

*Extension:* Use the printed papers as placemats at snacktime.

## Star Necklaces

Cut star shapes out of heavy paper using the pattern on page 143 as a guide. Write a child's name on each star. Give your children their stars. Have them trace their names and around the edges of their stars with glue. Then let them sprinkle glitter over the glue. Have them shake the excess glitter into a box. Punch a hole in the top of each child's star and put it on a long piece of yarn to make a necklace.

*Extension*: Hang the star necklaces around the room. Have your children look for their stars as they "wonder where they are." When each child has found his or her star, recite or sing "Twinkle, Twinkle, Little Star" together.

## Four Little Stars

Use the pattern on page 143 to cut four star shapes out of felt. Place the stars on a flannelboard. As you recite the following poem, remove the stars one at a time.

Four little stars
Winking at me,
One shot off,
Then there were three.

Three little stars
With nothing to do,
One shot off,
Then there were two.

Two little stars
Afraid of the sun,
One shot off,
Then there was one.

One little star
Not having any fun,
It shot off,
Then there were none.

*Jean Warren*

## Flannelboard Fun

Photocopy the patterns on pages 142 and cut them out. If desired, cover them with clear self-stick paper. Attach strips of felt to the backs of the patterns. As you recite the rhyme "Twinkle, Twinkle, Little Star" with your children, place the patterns on a flannelboard.

## Star Matching Game

Out of heavy paper, cut pairs of stars with varying numbers of points. Mix up the pairs and set them out. Let your children take turns finding the matching star pairs by feeling, looking at and counting the points on the stars.

## Bright and Dim

Play this star-finding version of Hot and Cold with your children. Use the pattern on page 143 as a guide for cutting a star shape out of cardboard. Cover the star with foil. Have your children sit in a circle. Choose one child to be the Star Finder. Ask that child to close his or her eyes while you hide the foil-covered star in the room. Then have the Star Finder open his or her eyes and look for the star. When the child gets close to the hidden star, have the other children say "bright." When the child gets farther away, have the children say "dim."

## There's a Tiny Little Star
Sung to: "Little White Duck"

There's a tiny little star
Way up in the sky,
A tiny little star,
Up so very high.
She twinkles brightly
Through the night,
But during the day
She is out of sight.
There's a tiny little star,
Way up in the sky.
A tiny little star.

*Jean Warren*

## Star Snacks

Serve your children slices of star fruit on paper plates cut into star shapes. Or serve star-shaped crackers. Or use small, star-shaped cookie cutters to cut stars out of cheese slices.

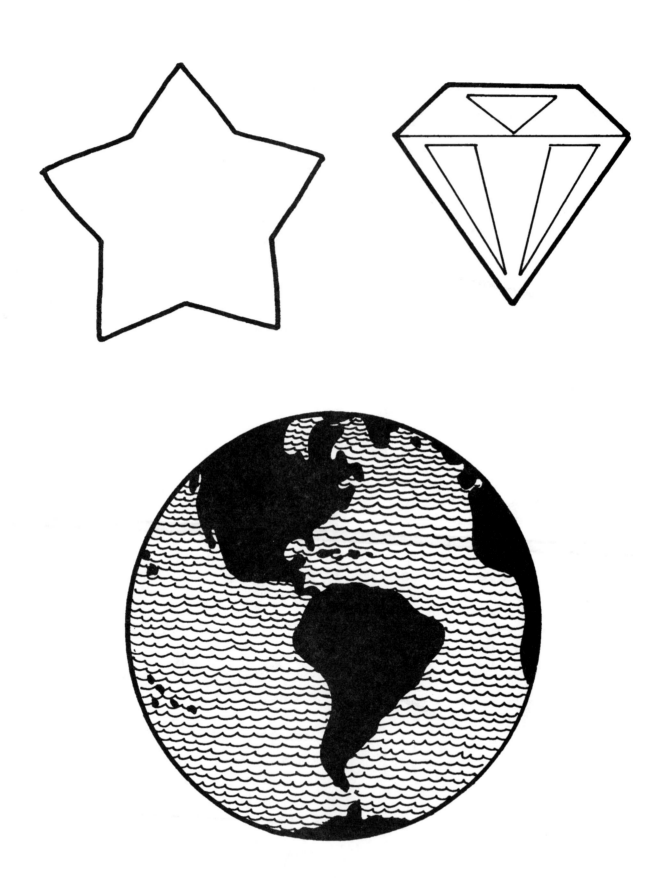

# Wee Willie Winkie

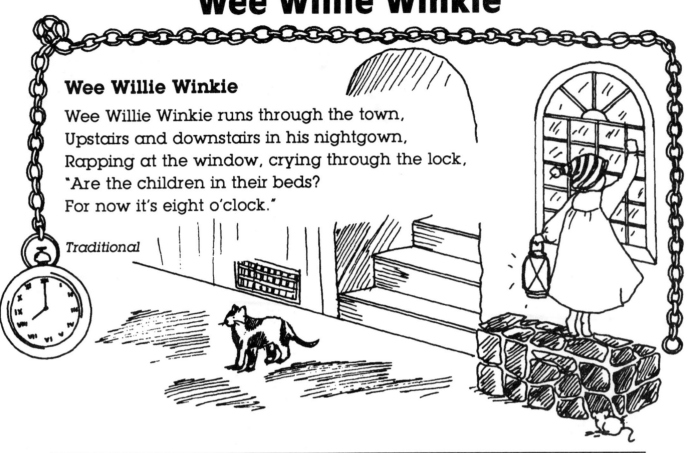

### Wee Willie Winkie

Wee Willie Winkie runs through the town,
Upstairs and downstairs in his nightgown,
Rapping at the window, crying through the lock,
"Are the children in their beds?
For now it's eight o'clock."

*Traditional*

### Night Sky Art

Give each of your children a white crayon and a white piece of construction paper. Let your children use their crayons to draw night sky pictures on their papers. (Have them press down hard with their crayons.) Then set out brushes and black tempera paint thinned with water to make a wash. Have the children brush the tempera wash over their pictures to turn them into Night Sky Art.

## Peeking Through Keyholes

Give each of your children an index card with a keyhole cut out of the center. Have the children look through the keyholes in their cards and tell you what they see.

## Flannelboard Fun

Photocopy the patterns on pages 148 and 149 and cut them out. If desired, cover them with clear self-stick paper. Attach strips of felt to the backs of the patterns. Place the patterns on a flannelboard. As you recite the rhyme "Wee Willie Winkie" with your children, move Wee Willie Winkie up and down the stairs and to the window and the door of the house.

## Making Stairs

Cut the following sizes of strips out of cardboard: 1- by 6-inch, 1- by 5-inch, 1- by 4-inch, 1- by 3-inch, 1- by 2-inch and 1- by 1-inch. Let your children take turns arranging the strips on a table to make a staircase with the longest strip on the bottom, the shortest strip on the top and one side lined up evenly.

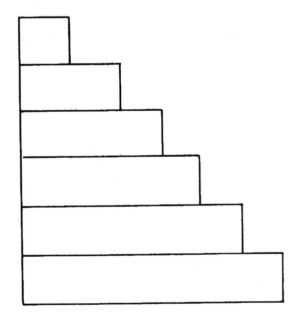

## Pajama Day

Have a Pajama Day! Let all of your children wear their pajamas. Encourage them to bring their favorite blankets, stuffed animals or bedtime stories. Have a relay race for dressing and undressing a teddy bear for bed.

## Wee Willie Winkie Obstacle Course

Set up an obstacle course for your children. Try to include some stairs to walk up and down and a door to go through. Give your children night caps to wear on their heads and flashlights. Dim the room lights. (Be sure there is still enough light for safe movement.) Let your children pretend to be Wee Willie Winkie walking through the streets at night as they go through the obstacle course.

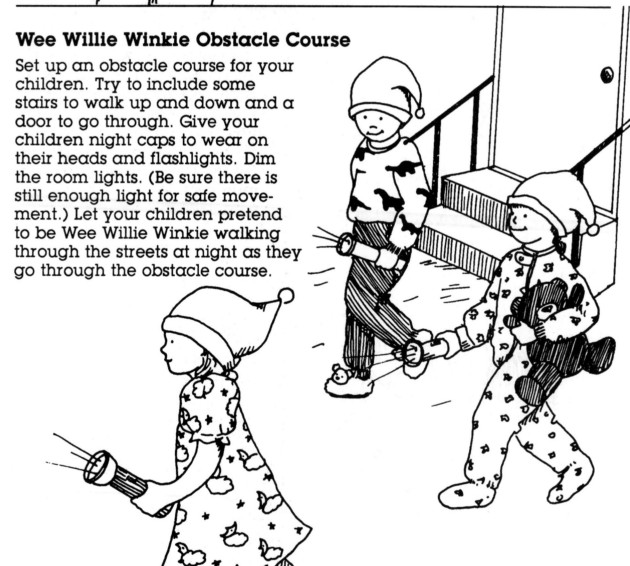

## Rapping Game

Have your children rap their fists on the floor or a table as you say the following chant out loud.

One rap, two rap, three rap, four,
Who's that rapping at my door?

Five rap, six rap, seven rap, eight,
Don't you think it's kind of late?

*Jean Warren*

## Go to Sleep Now
Sung to: "Frere Jacques"

Go to sleep now,
No eyes peek now,
Close your eyes,
Close them tight.
Dreaming, you will soon be,
Oh, the things you will see.
Sweet, sweet dreams,
Sweet, sweet dreams.

Have your children pretend to sleep as you sing.

*Bobbie Lee Wagman*

**148** Wee Willie Winkie

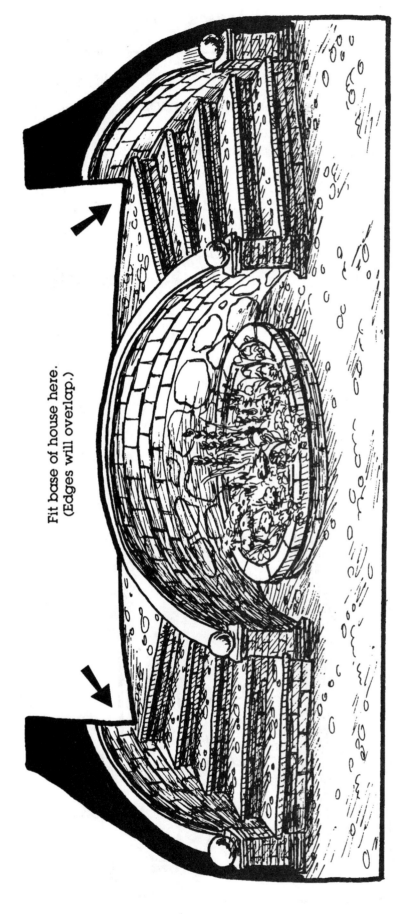

Fit base of house here.
(Edges will overlap.)

# Nursery Rhyme Review

## Nursery Rhyme Names

Print the names of nursery rhyme characters on self-stick labels. Give each of your children a label to wear at circle time. Address each child by his or her character name.

## Rhyming Words

Every nursery rhyme can be a language activity. After reciting a rhyme over several days, pause as you reach the end of a line to let your children finish with the rhyming word. For example: "Jack and Jill went up the _____."

## Nursery Rhyme Riddles

After your children are familiar with nursery rhymes, read them some of the following riddles. (Or make up some of your own.) Have them try to guess which nursery rhyme characters are being described.

I went to school.
My lamb followed me.
  (Mary.)

We went to the well.
We fell down the hill.
  (Jack and Jill.)

I'm nimble and quick.
I jumped over a candlestick.
  (Jack.)

I sat on a wall.
When I fell off the wall, I broke.
  (Humpty Dumpty.)

I blow my horn to call the sheep.
I fell asleep under the haystack.
  (Little Boy Blue.)

## Nursery Rhyme Bag

Collect objects that represent various nursery rhymes and put them in a bag. Have your children sit in a circle. Let them take turns reaching into the bag, pulling out an object and guessing which rhyme it represents. Then recite that rhyme together.

## Nursery Rhyme Windows

Tape a row of clear-plastic photo holders down each side of a large sheet of posterboard. Attach a metal paper fastener next to each photo holder, toward the center of the board. Cut index cards to fit inside the photo holders. Print or draw nursery rhyme go-togethers on pairs of index cards. For example, draw the Queen of Hearts and some tarts, the numerals 1 and 2 and a buckled shoe, Peter and a pumpkin, etc. Put one of each pair in the left-hand column of photo holders. Put the remaining cards in random order in the right-hand column. Tie short pieces of yarn to the paper fasteners on the left.

Then let the children match the cards by winding the loose ends of the yarn pieces around the appropriate paper fast-eners on the right. Change the cards in the photo holders as desired to review different nursery rhymes.

## Concentration Game

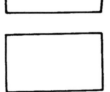
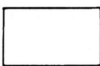

Divide 12 index cards into pairs. On each pair draw the same simple picture of a nursery rhyme character. Mix up all the cards and place them face down on the floor. Let one of your children begin by turning up two cards. If the pictures match, let the child keep the cards. If the pictures do not match, have the child replace both cards face down exactly where they were before. Continue the game until all the cards have been matched. Let the child with the most matched cards have the first turn when you start the game again.

## Nursery Rhyme Treasure Hunt

Set out clues for a Nursery Rhyme Treasure Hunt. Use clues such as these: "This was buckled. Jack and Jill went to get this. This struck one." Hide the clues in the appropriate places, then help your children go on their treasure hunt. Make the last clue lead the children to a special nursery rhyme treat such as pease porridge or Queen of Hearts tarts.

## Costume Day

Collect a variety of dress-up clothes and props that relate to nursery rhymes and their characters. For example, you could have mouse ears, a water bucket, a candlestick, a stuffed toy lamb, a cooking pot, shoes that buckle, etc. Let your children use the clothes and props to pretend they are different nursery rhyme characters. Encourage them to act out the rhymes with each other.

## Tube Town Characters

Use toilet tissue tubes as stands for cutouts of your favorite nursery rhyme characters. On one end of each tube, cut two ½-inch slits on either side. Photocopy the desired nursery rhyme character patterns from this book and mount them on heavy paper. (Or draw simple pictures of the desired characters on heavy paper.) Decorate the characters and then place them in the slits of the tubes to make them stand up.

## Nursery Rhyme Scrapbook

On large pieces of construction paper, write out the rhymes your children know. Let your children decorate each page with drawings, stickers or glued-on magazine pictures. Then let them look through their scrapbook and "read" the rhymes to one another.

## Nursery Rhyme Tree

Stand a tree branch in a pot of soil. Collect a variety of small objects mentioned in nursery rhymes and hang them from the branch. For example, a child's buckled shoe for "One, Two, Buckle My Shoe"; a toy horn or horn ornament for "Little Boy Blue"; some black yarn for "Baa, Baa Black Sheep". Have your children guess which objects go with which nursery rhymes. Then let your children find other items to hang from your Nursery Rhyme Tree.

## Famous Pairs Matching Game

Think of pairs of nursery rhyme characters, such as Mary and her lamb, Jack and Jill, Miss Muffet and the spider, etc. Draw a simple picture of each character on an index card. Mix up the cards and let your children take turns matching the nursery rhyme pairs.

## Nursery Rhyme Sequence Cards

Select a nursery rhyme that tells a story such as "Jack and Jill" or "Humpty Dumpty." Choose four or five events from the rhyme and draw a simple picture representing each event on a separate index card. For example, if you choose "Jack and Jill" you could draw Jack and Jill walking up a hill, Jack and Jill with a pail of water, Jack falling down and Jill falling down. Then mix up the cards and let your children take turns placing them in order.

## Nursery Rhyme Pantomimes

Set out illustrations of familiar nursery rhymes. Choose two of your children to select one of the pictures and have them act out that rhyme. Let the other children try to guess which rhyme it is. Repeat until everyone has had a turn.

## My Favorite Rhyme
Sung to: "Mary Had a Little Lamb"

The rhyme I love the very best,
Very best, very best,
The rhyme I love the very best
Is Mary Had a Little Lamb.

Substitute other nursery rhymes for
*Mary Had a Little Lamb.*

*Jean Warren*

## Raise Your Hand
Sung to: "If You're Happy and You Know It"

If you know Humpty Dumpty,
Raise your hand.
If you know Humpty Dumpty,
Raise your hand.
If you know this rhyme today,
Then you can help me say,
All the words to Humpty Dumpty today.

Substitute other nursery rhymes for *Humpty Dumpty.*

*Jean Warren*

# If you like Totline® Books, you'll love Totline® Magazine!

**Totline**
MAGAZINE
**Active preschool learning at its best**

Flying
High with
Windy Day
Fun

Focus on
**Eyes**
Activities
Worth a Look

**Discovering
Purple**

SHE'S COLORING ON MY PAPER!
**Problem-Solving Tips**

**F**or fresh ideas that challenge and engage young children in active learning, reach for **Totline Magazine**—Proven ideas from innovative teachers!

## Each issue includes

- Seasonal learning themes
- Stories, songs, and rhymes
- Open-ended art projects
- Science explorations
- Reproducible parent pages
- Ready-made teaching materials
- Activities just for toddlers
- Reproducible healthy snack recipes
- Special pull-outs